I0634360

William À Beckett

The earl's choice and other poems

William À Beckett

The earl's choice and other poems

ISBN/EAN: 9783337206758

Printed in Europe, USA, Canada, Australia, Japan

Cover: Foto ©Andreas Hilbeck / pixelio.de

More available books at **www.hansebooks.com**

CONTENTS.

—◦⟨◦⟩◦—

a 3

PREFACE.

MANY of the following poems were written years ago—contemporaneously, or nearly so, with the events and feelings that gave rise to their composition. The "Earl's Choice," which ought perhaps to be designated a tale in verse, rather than a poem, is of recent production. So also are the Sonnets; and some of the Minor Poems will afford internal evidence of having been written after the Author's final return to England. During his residence in Australia (1837-58), he was too much engaged in the pursuit of his profession, to allow of frequent intercourse with the Muse; but although thus debarred the poet's vocation, the aspirations of one never forsook him, and resulted, from time to time, in those utterances from which the present selection is made. To the earliest of these he has affixed dates; the remainder are located amid his more recent effusions without specification, and in an order irrespective of their chronological sequence.

Some of the poems thus selected may be thought too personal for the public eye ; but however amenable to critical objection on that account, the Author feels assured that they will not be the less acceptable to the circle in which they will probably find their chief circulation. To the general reader, indeed, unaccredited verse of any sort appeals with small chance of welcome ; and in no expectation that his own will form an exception, has the Author published the present volume. He believes that the friends who look for it will give it kindly greeting, and he knows that those, nearer and dearer than friends, will be thankful for a more durable memorial of his thoughts and feelings than would remain to them in the fragile and disjointed leaves of unrevised manuscript. Such a memorial he leaves to them in the volume now published, and to them he dedicates what by them will be best appreciated.

Surbiton, January, 1863.

THE EARL'S CHOICE.

A Tale in Verse.

IN SIX PARTS.

THE EARL'S CHOICE.

PROEM.

HERE is no tale of knightly chivalry,
No fabulous or legendary lay,
No golden picture of the " Good old Times,"
But a most homely story of our own,
Unaided by " effects sensational,"
And fashioned in quite unromantic shape.
No tale is it of the impossible,
Or e'en the marvellous ; to bards of more
Ambitious aim I leave that bolder flight
Which soars above the dull routine of earth
In quest of the heroic ; content am I
With what of good or lofty may be traced
Amid the paths where human footsteps walk
Their daily round ; where man his fellow meets,
Nor in him finds an angel or a fiend.

Here is no picture of ideal men
Among ideal women—both doing deeds
That man nor woman ever did before :
The truthful present from the doubtful past
Calls me away ; my Muse is of the earth,
And, thence invoked, she bids me sing no song
(Albeit sung in transcendental strain)
That would appeal to human ears or hearts,
Which wakes not also human sympathies.

But e'en from earth some heavenly feelings spring,
And my tale is of *one ;* from loftiest bard
What song, this wanting, were of audience sure ?
Yet am I rash to think it may be sung—
This holiest passion that our nature knows—
With none of that contaminating gloss,
With none of those vile intermixtures which
Blend love with folly, wickedness, or shame ?
Rash to believe, at least, that to *one* sex,
Without such stain, my song will welcome prove,
Moving, perchance, some gentle lips to say,
(If gentle eyes this page should ever greet,)
" Here is a lay that maid or wife may read,
And from the reading rise without a blush."

Yet, were I faithless to my own design,
Light were the blame compared with that incurred
By one to whom the admiring age accords
The poet's bay ; when minstrel such as he

Befouls the purer current of his verse
With tuneful warblings of a wanton's wiles,
And wife's deceit—when he, around whose harp
The fair and young in listening homage sit,
Hanging impatient on his every word,
Allows such unmeet utterance to go forth,
Speaking of vices which no maid should know,
Speaking of frailties which no maid should hear,
He does a harm beyond my power to work,
Fails in the high example he should set,
Leads where 'tis base to follow, and prepares
A shadow for his genius and his fame.

"To labour is to pray." The saying's old,
And in these days has grown into a creed,
Which all with lips—if not with heart—profess:
It is the doctrine of the haughty peer,
And wealthy commoner; the kings of trade
Proclaim it, and the meanest artisan
Adopts it, oft, to fling it back in scorn
On those from whom it came; the demagogue
Confronts with it the proud aristocrat,
Who, in his turn, for purpose of his own,
Swears by the adage to applauding mobs.
Alike in pulpit, and on platform preached,
It comes commended from the lips of priests,
Saints, patriots, politicians; thus 'twould seem,
Whatever else may yet be in dispute
In this most Christian and enlightened land,

That " work is worship " is a truth agreed.
Well, let us call it worship, but of Whom ?
How much belongs to Mammon, and how much
To Bacchus, in the busy marts of work ?
And what's there holy in that drudgery
Which fits the soul for neither Earth nor Heaven ?
" Worship," no more let's desecrate the word,
Nor go on calling by exalted names
Things but of mean or sad significance.
There is but one ennobling work for man,
Or woman either—that which Duty wills
And executes ; whenever *that* is done,
By prince or peasant, or by head or hand,
'Tis nobly done, and work *is* worship there.
For work like this, all have necessity,
The high and low, the rich and poor alike,
Are called to it.   Much talk has lately been
Of Woman's work—of what it should *not* be,
And what it *should :* but all the talk has been
Of woman struggling for her daily bread ;
As if the one to rank and affluence born
Nor need nor obligation had for work.
What—whilst her lowlier sister's hard-tasked life
From morn to night is one continued toil,
With no sweet use of body, mind, or heart,
Is she with time and means at her command
For ordering these as suits her whim or will,
To use them but as servile ministers
Of ease and pleasure from her birth to death ?

Is she to no more high vocation called
Than to take counsel of her milliner
How she may shine at opera or ball ?
In what attire to sit her ottoman,
Her chariot, or her steed ?—how deck herself
For exhibition at some fancy fair ?
Or how her pretty hand had best be gloved
To take her prayer-book from the liveried slave
Standing, with powdered head, and well-turned calf,
To wait on her, ere waiting on his God ?
Or let us place her in a lower rank—
Offspring of parent who to industry
In trade or commerce owes the wealth by which
He rears his daughter in such careful way
As that she may, unchallenged, stand among
The ladies of the land.   What is *her* work ?
Has *she* no call upon her faculties
Higher than what may fitting answer find
In mastery of such accomplishments
As music, drawing, dancing-masters teach ?
Let these not be disdained, nor let her shun
The needle, whether for its grace or use,
Nor spurn, indeed, the aid of any art
That innocently to her person brings
An added charm, or gifts her with the power
Of pleasing others by her tutored skill.
Yet small the worth of such proficiency
Without due culture of the mind and heart ;
Add that she's maiden of a serious turn,

Frequents the church, attends at Sunday schools,
Distributes tracts, pays visits to the poor,
From waltzing shrinks, to theatres ne'er goes,
And in the parson puts her firmest faith !
What then—if she from no inspiring sense
Of duty such description earns ; if all
This occupation's but for fashion's sake,
The copying of a pattern which she follows
Because 'tis set, or haply offers her
Convenient vent for sensibilities
That cost no self-denial to indulge—
If in her ministrations to the poor,
Whether in aid of body, or of soul,
She can but echo what another says,
And to each varying want, and varying woe,
That meet her in her periodic rounds,
Comes with the self-same face and self-same words,
Her charity is but a cold routine,
And she, at best, but an automaton,
Moved to her work by artificial springs.
Yet better this than sitting still at home
In sentimental dream, or pillowing
In idle ease upon her silken lap
Some pious novel, or exciting tale,
Which leave her weaker than she was before
For strength of purpose, and for truth of act.
Better a night at opera or ball
Than day of morbid reverie—better aught
Of life and action in the busy world,

With heart alive to others' joys and griefs,
Than only sensitive to those of fiction,
Or brooding selfishly upon her own.

O sex of which it is the Briton's boast
That, in his land, thy noblest image dwells,
Believing with a fervent faith that *there*
Woman is dearest, purest, fairest found—
Domestic idol of each lordly home
And lowly cot—whate'er thy station be—
Above it, e'er remember, is *thyself!*
The " wheel of fortune neither love nor hate,"
And thou, dear lady, who art placed above
The wants that bow thy humbler sister down,
And tastest joys which she may never know,
Make not the barrier wider than it is
'Twixt her and thee, by apathy or scorn;
Let not the icy breath of Custom chill
Thy woman's heart, nor its imperious tone
Silence the voice of thy diviner mind:
Spite of the bonds in which it strives to hold thee,
And of the worship which the world demands
From *all* for this its idol; no more respect
Do thou, than may become a gentle heart
And honest mind, accord it; its fit due
Rightly discerning, pay; nay, e'en allow
Occasional exactions—for to yield,
In naught that injures truth or modesty,
Rather than, by resistance, harsh remark

Or misconstruction risk, were wisdom's part.
But never let its menace scare thy soul
From off its pedestal, nor there to swerve
Beyond its balance ; despot though it be
Of power almost omnipotent, should it dare
Wrong to thyself or others' counsel, defy it,
And He, who is Omnipotence entire,
Shall come beside thee with a viewless strength,
And steady thee with his Almighty arm,
Till thou shalt stand more firmly fixed than ever
Against the aim of every hostile shaft
That would detach thee from thy chosen height.

Woman at once thus gentle, and thus strong,
Thus bending and thus firm ; with heart informed
By deeper, tenderer sensibilities
Than tracts or novels teach—with mind prepared
By discipline, and culture, to recoil
From all there seeking entrance that wears not
Some impress of the beautiful and true ;
Subject, not slave, to laws conventional
(Where reverence for no higher law demands
Rebellion) ; masculine alone in will ;
Serenely treading wheresoe'er her path ;
Not murmuring, whate'er its roughness be,
But stooping, meekly, to remove its thorns,
Rather than step aside to look for flowers
Which spring not in her way ; more apt, perchance,
To weep than smile ; content, yet blushing not

To own, if maiden, to the maiden's hope
Of lying some day on a husband's breast ;
But, wed or unwed, cheerful-hearted still,
And ever mindful of the simple creed,
Whate'er her fortune or her fate may be,
That peace and happiness can only come
From duty well perceived, and well performed :—
Woman like this—if to her nobler traits
Be added cultured mind, and manners fraught
With gentle dignity and graceful ease,
Is stamped the *lady* by a higher right
Than birth, wealth, rank, or all combined, confer.
Woman like this I sing—no heroine
For a " Strange Story " or exciting tale ;
Too unideal for the bard sublime,
But dearly welcome to my humble Muse.

PART I.

An Artist's room in London—it is night,
And the pale lamp, by which the Artist sits,
Gazing upon the portrait on his easel,
Shows little of the workman or his work.
Holding the door of an adjoining chamber
A maiden stands, watching the portrait too;
Then, with a sigh she struggles to suppress,
Advances to the silent sitter, and
With hand upon his shoulder softly speaks—
"Eustace! 'tis late, I'd have some talk with you
Before you go to rest, will you come now?
I would have asked you earlier, but I saw
Whose portrait was before you, and I feared
To break the dream in which you seemed enwrapped
While gazing on it; but come now; 'tis late,
And chilly here; our fire is still alight,
And it distresses me to see you thus;
Come, Eustace!"   At that gentle voice, he turned,
And, rising, took the lamp to follow her,
Exclaiming, as its light fell on the face
From which he seemed reluctant still to move,
"Oh, wretched waste of head, and hand, and heart!"

They sat them down, the brother and the sister,
Beside their mutual hearth; speechless awhile,
Not from reserve, but tender reticence
Of words which spoke by either must give pain :
At length Lucille (so called he her) began—
"Eustace, will you forgive me, if I say
That this dejection is unmanning you ;
Why *should* you waste your head, and hand, and heart ?
Did you not think I heard you say those words ?"

"Lucille," he quick returned—"had I possessed
Your coldness, or your courage, or your pride,
I had escaped this blight that is upon me,
You should have had my nature, and I yours ;
Then, with a broken heart, I might have still
With steady hand, and smiling eye, pursued
The art that has undone me ; you will say
That fame and fortune are at my command,
Having achieved so much beyond my hopes ;
But what are fame and fortune without love ?
What Art itself without *that* inspiration ?
You'll tell me soon this is but woman's talk,
But, if I dare to say I am a man
In your stern presence, I am here to prove
'Tis what a *man* can feel."

"Oh, Eustace ! Eustace !"
(And the tears started as she thus replied)—
"Your sadness makes you angry and unkind ;

You would not speak so if you were yourself,
You would not speak so if you read aright
The heart whose very womanhood you doubt :
Whate'er *my* heart is, shall I see your own
Writhe, like Laocoon, in the serpent's coil,
Beneath the torture of a hopeless passion,
And not attempt to free you from its folds—
To strangle it before it strangles you ?—
Were *that* a sister's part ?"

                                    " Well—not to-night,"
Said Eustace kindly, " let us further talk,
For, as you say, I am not quite myself,
And do not think I e'er shall be again
What I once was—perchance with time—ah me !
Good night !" She kissed him, and replied—" Good
     night."

    And so to rest they went; with heavy hearts,
But not uncomforted by prayer to Him
On whom, though neither spoke of, both reclined ;
For they had grown together in a faith
Matured to firm conviction in the soil
Of free inquiry; doubts, and hopes, and fears,
Had once been theirs in every varied hue
And gloom that fleck the intellectual air ;
But now the sky above their souls was clear,
And, whate'er shadow rose between themselves,
None ever came betwixt them and their God.

Their grief, we may be sure, was told to Him
Before they courted sleep ; and let none doubt
The soothing answer, which they sought for, came—
The peace vouchsafed to every sorrowing heart
Not barred against its entrance by remorse.
Let them sleep on—the while my verse relates
Some portion of their earlier history.

Twin children were they of departed parents,
Orphaned when scarce beyond their infancy.
I dare not say they were of gentle blood,
For (let it not shock sentimental ears)
It must be owned their father, though called by
The euphonious name of Grantley, earned his bread
By trade,—which swamps gentility at once,
Save when the tradesman dies a millionnaire,
Leaving sufficient to keep down the word
In people's memories, or, at least, their tongues,
In servile compliment to some young heir,
Who, grown ashamed of shop or counting-house,
From Eton fresh, or Oxford, cuts Cornhill
To figure in Pall Mall and Rotten-Row.
But our twins' sire had not gone out of life
With such *éclat*. The pittance he bequeathed
Was scarcely worth the trouble of a search
At Doctors' Commons by a prying press ;
Though, with good care, 'twas found to be enough
To rear his offspring in that gentle breeding
Which is more precious far than gentle birth,

Or titled wealth.　　Their home was 'neath the roof
Of a fond uncle, their sole guardian left,
A pensioned Indian judge—of tastes refined,
And mind whose cultivation never ceased
Till life ceased also ; his whole heart and soul
He gave to rearing up his orphan wards,
Shaping their minds and manners in a mould
That fitted them for nobler life than standing,
Like well-draped statues, on their pedestals,
Unfit for contact with the breathing world.
To manhood one, to womanhood the other,
Grew with maturing consciousness in each
Of the eternal warfare to be waged
'Twixt high and low desire ; this, early felt,
Was ne'er forgotten.　　When they came of age,
Their guardian, 'neath whose roof they still remained,
Witnessed the seed he'd planted bearing fruit
Of promise rare ; and when he died, soon after,
'Twas with conviction both would keep the path
They had so firmly trod within his view.
They mourned his death with many a grateful tear
Of love and reverence ; and, at first, they felt
Their lonely independence as a weight
Grievous to bear.　　Kind offers to Lucille
Came, from some friends, of temporary home ;
Others, in doubt of what her means might be,
Hinted that, with her known accomplishments,
Her income might be doubled, would she choose
To turn them to account ; and one proud dame,

Who was astonished that " a tradesman's daughter
Had such an air *distingué*," and who vowed
" Her voice would make her fortune on the stage,"
Offered, " if she were really in distress,"
To take her as companion. What was best—
Mid this unlooked-for medley of advice
And curious solicitude—to do ?
Their uncle's will had so increased their means,
As left them free to independent action.
To dwell together was their first resolve ;
Next, that the art which had been Grantley's choice,
And, in his uncle's lifetime, he had studied,
Should, after two years' residence in Rome,
Be his profession. This resolved, was done.
The two years over, they returned to England,
Each in their several and their mutual tastes
With added knowledge and with added skill.

A year had passed since they had fixed their home
Where we had left them sleeping ; in that time
Grantley, who came from Rome with much repute,
No lack of sitters had ; but his chief fame
Rose from two pictures for the public eye—
" Juliet's night colloquy with Romeo ; "
And, from the *Winter's Tale*, the " Statue Scene."
Both had been purchased by a rich young peer,
Causing much talk amid his noble friends ;
Whilst, of the " Juliet," the critics said
That, in our galleries, seldom had been seen
Beauty so rare portrayed by art so fine.

The pictures to their owner's country mansion
Had been conveyed—to Castle Valmont, where
The young Earl chiefly dwelt—example fair
To all around ; son of a mother proud
Of him, more of his rank ; need it be said
How many other mothers had been glad
To see their child his bride ? but rumour went,
Amid the circles which such gossip moved,
That young Lord Valmont was no marrying man ;
Which meant, perchance, he had not yet been trapped
Into proposal for a wife. Some said
He loved beneath his rank, but that his pride
Still kept him single ; all declared 'twas time,
Tho' not yet twenty-eight, that he was wed ;
And e'en his sister, who seemed dearer to him
Than any other of her sex, would sometimes ask—
Half jest, half earnest, "If he had resolved
To die a bachelor ? " One day, she came
Into the room where hung the "Juliet,"
And found him gazing on it with an air
Of wrapped abstraction till, as she approached,
" Clara," he said, " you've asked me many times
If I am sworn to die a bachelor,
Show me a face like *that*, and I will wed."
" A lovely face—a very lovely face ! "
Said Clara, eyeing it attentively,
" And yet, perchance, the same in flesh and blood
You'd hold but commonplace—I could point out
A score of Juliets that are quite as fair

And yet attract no notice from your eye;
But let me place one of them on that canvas,
Sky, moonlight, garden, balcony,—as there,
And she herself portrayed with equal skill,
And, tho' the self-same face you'd seen before,
A hundred times, without a second look,—
You'd gazing stand, as now you gaze on this,
Till you had wrought yourself to the belief
The world could show none like it."

       " Sister dear,"

Replied the Earl, in almost serious tone—
" I have not said that I shall never wed,
Because I've found not—and may never find—
My heart's ideal; but in such a face
As *that* I hope to find it, if at all.
I know the Juliets *you* have in your eye,
But none of them, that e'er attracted mine,
Had aught that painter, were he Raphael's self
And truthful to his art, could so depict
As to reflect the charms that I admire
In her on yonder canvas; you may smile
And tell me, as you did the other day,
That, could I see the fair original,
'Twould prove to be some mindless peasant girl
Picked up amid the wilds of Italy,
Or in the suburbs of its capital,
Where twenty such might any day be seen.
'Tis one, be sure, for which no model sat

Save the one visioned to the artist's eye;
'Tis some ideal which absorbs his mind,
And ineffaceably possesses him.
For mark the features of Hermione
In the companion picture, and you'll see,
Despite the obvious difference of the two,
In *that* the calm and stately matron standing,
Suppressing all that moves her faithful heart,
That she may seem the statue which she feigns;
In *this* the maiden, confidently fond,
Breathing her love with gushing unreserve—
That but *one face* was in the artist's mind.
By the way, Clara, has my mother told you
What made him quit, so suddenly, our roof?
I asked her how it happened, and she says—
'No matter, 'tis as well that he is gone;
Painters, whate'er their talents, are not guests
For peers.' She has, I fear, offended him
By some such hint; can you enlighten me?"

    Clara's reply was almost with a blush—
"You know our mother's more than haughty way
To all she deems beneath her: well—I strove,
During your absence, to be kind and courteous
Unto the guest you had invited here,
Tho' 'a mere painter' as my mother called him.
And hence what followed—for she observing this,
Grew wroth with me, and haughtier with him;
Forbade, when he was sketching in the park,

Or painting in the gallery, that I
Should notice or address him, till at length
Pending some touches to my portrait, she
Startled us both by this strange exclamation :
'Pray, Mr. Grantley, do you stare at *all*
Your sitters in that fashion?' He arose,
And saying, 'Madam, I will stare no more,'
Went from the chamber. After he had gone,
'Mother,' I said, 'you make me blush for you.'
'Blush for yourself,' she cried; 'don't tell me, Clara,
Artist or not, he'd eye you as he did
Without encouragement!' I spoke some words
Which sent her fiercely flashing from the room,
Leaving me there, when suddenly, the door
Opened again, and Grantley, calmly walking
Up to the easel, took my portrait from it,
Exclaiming, 'Lady, if I ever dared
To let one glance fall otherwise on thee
Than spake such homage as all eyes must pay
Which look on face so fair; if e'er mine eye
Essayed to thine conveyance of one thought
Unworthy of true gentleman to harbour
(And none more true does your proud mother know,
Whate'er his rank, that comes to Castle Valmont),
Forgive me ere I go.' 'Indeed,' said I,
'There's no forgiveness needed; pray forget
My mother's words, or if you will depart
Leave me my portrait.' Bowing, he replied,
'It needs some touches yet, none that require

Your presence more ; of mine I now relieve you ;'
And in this mood he left ; no more I know."

   " Strange in my mother, strange in Grantley, too,"
Said Valmont, at the close of this recital.
" Why should he take your portrait ? when I left,
'Twas nearly finished ; things must not rest thus.
Clara, I shall invite him to return,
If *you* have no objection ? "

                        " None ; why should I ? "
Clara replied ; " but what if he declines ?
If I have read his character aright,
You'll never see him more at Castle Valmont."

   " Indeed," retorted Valmont, somewhat sharply,
" Are you so quick at catching character ?
Or have you special aptitude for finding
What constitutes the artist's ?—his, at least,
Who paints your pretty face, and takes it home,
That he may look upon it as he'd like
To look on the original !   Nay, Clara,
Don't flush and fume—I only spoke in jest ;
I know this Grantley is no common man,
Nor common artist, and I grieve with you
His feelings should be wounded 'neath our roof."

   But what *were* Grantley's feelings ?—warmer far
Than Lady Clara or her brother guessed.

The shrewd cold Countess had interpreted
Coarsely, but not quite falsely, as he hung
Upon her daughter's every look and word,
Feeding upon them with an appetite
That hourly keener grew.   In hints at first
She vented her displeasure, till at length
The climax came, as we have heard it told.
Not unexpected was it by Lucille.
Grantley had writ to her, from time to time,
Telling her all that he had thought and felt ;
How that the Lady Clara, who had been
So courteous to him in his studio,
Was still more courteous in her own proud halls,
Greeting him always with a kind regard,
Whether alone, or mid gay company—
The same in simplest garb or richest robe—
And every day some added charm revealing,
Some grace or beauty, scarcely marked at first,
But stealing on the mind with frequent view,
Till there imprinted ineffaceably ;
Like those fine touches in Art's noblest works,
Which, missing recognition when first seen,
O'ertake at last the wrapped spectator's sense,
And dwell there evermore.   So Grantley wrote
Of her who had to his own pencil sat—
Portrayed as truly as the *hand* could show,
But which, he said, "failed in the power to trace
Her image in its mental loveliness,
Or as its radiance shone upon his heart."

Language like this unto Lucille. seemed proof
Of passion growing fast; and thus she wrote—
" Eustace, I feel 'tis time for me to speak
My honest thoughts of your fond eulogy.
You love the Lady Clara! Hopeless dream !
Dispel it, ere from thy o'erheated thoughts
It rise, a cloud with fatal lightning charged,
The heart it shades to shatter! She *your* wife ?
The world 'twixt you and her a gulf has fixed,
Which it were madness to attempt to bridge.
Attempt it not! You owe it to yourself—
You owe it—No! I will not make pretence
Of obligations which no warrant have
For imposition, but the servile creed
Which makes of rank a thing to be approached
With humble step, shy tongue, and fettered heart ;
Not in the common phrase such creed approves
Will I adjure thee, telling thee, forsooth,
That 'twere a base return for favour shown,
For patronage and hospitality,
To take advantage of your patron's trust
To win the fairest jewel of his house.
To such glib fallacies I give no heed,
Tho' current from long date, like other lies
That keep their footing, in obedience
To the almighty gospel of *May Fair*,
Which is not mine or thine ; no, 'tis for *you*—
For you alone I speak. Let the proud Earl,
His prouder mother, and her daughter fair,

Be their own guards of what the maid herself is
As free to give or to withhold, as you—
A cultured gentleman—are free to ask,
Tho' small your hope, and small your chance to win ;
For gentlemen who follow a vocation—
Albeit that of Titian or of Tully—
Small chance will have against the titled idlers
Mid whom earls' daughters love to find their mates.
So, brother mine, throw not away your love
On Lady Clara ; keep it to bestow
On her of whom you will not be too proud
To ask for love's return ; for who would risk
Contemptuous reply ?   Said I too *proud ?*
Nay, pride in such case were but self-respect.
Bow to the Lady Clara as she sits
Beside your canvas, as a worthy shrine
For incense of your genius ; yield her *that,*
The radiant homage of the artist's hand,
But free from worship of the artist's heart."

   Such letter had reached Grantley but an hour
Before the scene that led to his departure
From Castle Valmont.   In offended mood
He reached his home ; kissed hurriedly Lucille,
Who wondering stood at his abrupt return,
And then, revealing what had brought him back,
" Not," as he said, " her letter," sat him down
Sullenly in his studio, and besought
Lucille to leave him for awhile alone.

What further passed has been already told ;
'Twas the same night with which our tale began,
When, after words that had both deeply stirred,
Touching the love that Eustace had disclosed,
They went with fond, but heavy hearts, to rest.

PART II.

SOME days elapsed ere Grantley could resume
His wonted work.   Lucille, with gentle tact,
Cheered, soothed, advised him, yet still sad he was,
And oft sat brooding o'er the pictured face
From which she struggled to withdraw his thoughts.
'Twas now completed, but a duplicate,
More finished still, hung where it met his eye
At close and break of day; so thus he writes—
" My lord, the Lady Clara's portrait waits
To fill, at your command, its destined place."
Not many hours had sped his letter, ere
The Earl himself with kindly greeting came.
" Grantley," he said, " I'm vexed to find you here
'Stead of at Castle Valmont.   Let me beg
You will return; I have been told the cause
Of your departure, and am free to own
My mother's rudeness needs apology.
I'm loth to speak of what gave rise to it,
But let me, Grantley, give you my assurance
Of too entire reliance on your honour,
E'en were you rash enough to lose your heart,
To think you'd play the suitor to my sister."

" The *rashness* I admit," responded Grantley,
" But you'll forgive me if I fail to see
What *honour* has to do with it, my lord."

"Indeed," rejoined the Earl; "we'll put it thus, then—
You, my friend Grantley, find yourself received
In circles which you'll own above your station;
In circles which, you'll also own, do not
Furnish to tradesmen's sons their wives, or husbands
Unto their daughters.   Well, you enter them,
Are treated courteously; the friendship make
Of one, perchance, who much admires your art,
And, from respect both to it and yourself,
Invites you to pursue it 'neath his roof,
On equal terms with his own family
And other guests; in such a case, would you
Deem it no violation of the trust,
Implied, if not expressed, towards your host,
To make your art a stepping-stone to win
The affections of his daughter?"

                              "Put plausibly,
My lord," said Grantley; "but I answer thus—
That which it pleases you to call a *trust*,
And into obligation magnify,
As binding all who enter your charmed circle,
Is but assumption that the faith there held
Must be the faith of others; you rely
Upon the strength of barriers you've set up,

Because but rarely broken ; yet, my lord,
Within these barriers many born and bred
Are, sometimes, not less anxious to break out
Than those you deem invaders to break in.
Rebels or traitors call *them*, if you choose,
For breaking bonds imposed by no restraint,
Save those of pride and prejudice ; but I,
Who have not sworn allegiance to these laws,
Hold myself free to break them, if I dare,
Without the stigma, which your lordship hints,
Attaching to my honour.   Say it is
Presumption, impudence, audacity,
In the poor painter—guest of a rich earl,
To dream of wedding kith or kin of his ;
But if repeated intercourse with one
Should force him to discover that he loves her,
And to suspicion that she loves him too,
(Be there no difference but rank between them),
What in God's law forbids that they should pair ?
And, if they choose to brave the penalty
Of breaking laws conventional, to win
The happiness which such infraction brings,
Is it in either to be folly called,
In him dishonour, or in her disgrace ?
But to what purport is this talk, my lord ?
I have not put my theory to the test
Beneath your roof, altho' I gave no pledge
That I would not ; and I *do* love your sister.
Nay, do not frown, my lord, I have a right

To feel what I avow, though not, it seems,
To utter what I feel; but the avowal
Shall never reach *her* ear : you need not fear
The agony of having to endure
Too close alliance with a tradesman's son.
The Lady Clara may go free for me,
Tho' I have said, and say again—I love her."

" Grantley," the Earl, after a pause, replied,
" Your language takes me strangely by surprise,
And I confess is what I grieve to hear,
Both for your sake and mine ; but what has passed,
Though reason for your absence from my house,
Need put no barrier 'twixt yourself and me.
I'm sorry that my words have wounded you,
But feel assured, had you been in my place,
And I in yours, you would have said to me
Just what I've said to you ; if you could now
Be gifted with a dukedom, as I speak,
And had a sister, tell me honestly,
Would you consent, would she, that she should wed
A——"

" Tradesman's son. Don't spare the word, my lord,"
Responded Grantley ; " and my answer hear—
I *have* a sister, one who might ere now
Have found in rank a suitor for her hand,
Had she not proudly at due distance held it.
But were she a duke's daughter, and the man

She loved an upright cultured gentleman—
Whatever else he might be in the scale
Which weighs a man by what his father was—
She'd little heed ; but him alone would wed,
Tho' it should throw the fashionable world
Into convulsions."

   " Well," replied the Earl,
" Not to annoy you more, suppose we change
The subject. Can you finish here the sketches
Which you began ? and tell me, by the way
(I've often thought to ask you), is the face
Of Juliet in your picture from the life ? "
Grantley assenting, further said the Earl :
" So fair a face in life is rarely seen ;
It is a little flattered, I presume ?
Is she a lady ? "

   " *I* think so, my lord,"
Grantley replied, " if worth aught my opinion ;
But our ideas may differ on that point.
A lady 'tis that's very dear to me.
I told you just now that I had a sister—
The face is hers."

   " Indeed," replied the Earl ;
" Is it impertinent to ask if she
Resides with you ? " Ere answer came, the sound
Of a door opening made him turn his head

In the direction whence it came, and there
Emerging, 'neath the shadow of the curtain
Which hung across the portal, stood Lucille—
Who, at the sight of stranger with her brother,
Said, shrinking back, " I thought you were alone,"
Bowed slightly to the Earl, and then withdrew.
Grantley stood mute, and, with embarrassed look,
Turned to the Earl, who met him with these words—
" I need not ask you *who* that lady was.
Her portrait is not flattered; you can send
My sister's when you please.   Meantime, to yours
Make my apologies for keeping her
So long from your companionship.   Adieu ! "

On his departure came Lucille again.
" Eustace," she said, " I guess your visitor—
Lord Valmont, was it not ? "

                        " You guess aright,"
Said Grantley.   " Was it curiosity
That made you so impatient to behold him,
Or vanity that he in Juliet's face
Might recognize your own ?   Nay, don't look grave !
Forgive my badinage, and you shall hear
All that has passed between us ; but first say,
Now in the flesh that you have seen *his* face,
What think you of it, and then, sister mine,
I will inform you what he thinks of *yours*. "

Answered Lucille, " My thought no other is
Than when I saw his portrait. I then said,
He looks the nobleman in face and mind,
But face and mind are caught not at a glimpse ;
Therefore, how these might strike me in himself
I could not, without longer survey, tell."

" Discreetly answered, and you now shall hear,"
Said Grantley, " what this same most noble Earl
Thinks of us both ; for you not less than me
Our conference, ere ending, did concern."

Then all that passed he told her, word for word,
Lucille in silence listening to the close
Of his recital, holding in her heart
With difficult restraint ; until her tears,
Which had been rising fast with every word,
Echoed by Eustace, of that proud retort
Which followed on avowal of his love,
Burst forth at length with uncontrolled o'erflow,
And on his breast she fell with gasping breath,
Exclaiming, as she lay within his clasp,
" My own brave brother, you will conquer now."

Awhile in wordless sympathy they stood,
Till, said Lucille, " Put by your pencil now,
And come and lie down, whilst I sing to you
The song you wrote for me the other day ;
I have found out an air that suits it well.
Come ! "

Small persuasion needed he to go,
For the resolve to which he now stood pledged
Launched forth, in sudden impulse, from his heart,
Left it vibrating still with the recoil
Of its own blow; and all unfit to aid
In work of head or hand; so with Lucille
He from his studio, not reluctant, went,
And, resting on the couch near her piano,
Listened whilst she to an accordant air
These verses sang—

" Gaze with no tearful eye behind thee,
     Sighing can bring not the absent near,
 Nor would they care to sighing find thee,
     Present smiles are to them more dear.
 Why should farewells give birth to sorrow?
     What's life itself but one long adieu?
 When, oh, when, did the coming morrow
     Ever render the day's hopes true?

" Silence love's whispers firmly, boldly,
     Why should thy heart but beat to ache?
 Turn from the tempter, sternly, coldly,
     Who would its light in thy bosom wake.
 Keep on thy path unmoved, unshaken,
     Though thou shouldst die unloved, ungrieved;
 Better be lonely than forsaken,
     Better forsaken than deceived."

PART III.

THE time passed on, and Eustace, day by day,
Felt less and less the thraldom of his heart;
His palette now was rarely from his hand;
Work after work he finished; a design
He and Lucille had often talked of grew
Hourly beneath his touch, till soon both stood
Debating if, in aught, there might be change
Ere colour gave it life; the scene essayed
Was that where Paul before the Roman governor
Speaks till, as Scripture tells us, " Felix trembled."
" What I would show," said Grantley to Lucille,
" And you must tell me if I've failed, is this—
Truth in its majesty and moral might
Confounding human power—earthly judge
Trembling to hear a voice that seems to speak
Judgment divine—and shrinking from the words
As though from God's own lips—is all this here ? "
" I see enough to tell me that it will be,"
Smiling, replied Lucille; " when all is done
Which you, I know, can do; *then* doubt I not
To see, as clearly as you now describe,
The bright reality of your design."

So thus encouraged, on he bravely worked,
And felt, with every added touch, a glow
Of pride that made him glory in his art,
And envy none who knew not his vocation.

To Castle Valmont had its lord returned
To meet expected guests ; among them came
A certain kindly Marchioness who oft
At Rome had Grantley and his sister met.
She from the Countess-dowager now heard
Of his late stay, with hints of what had led
To his departure, and with view to probe
The Lady Clara for more full account,
Was soon beside her speaking to her thus—
"I find, my dear, you've had here on a visit—
Professional, I mean—that handsome man
And clever artist, Mr. Eustace Grantley.
What do you think of him ?   He and his sister
Were both in some sort protégés of mine
When wintering at Rome some two years since.
She sang delightfully, and he took portraits
Of our sweet sex in such enchanting style
That husbands fell in love a second time
At sight of their own wives ; and maids obtained
Admiring glances for their pictured faces
Which never met their own.   Yours, my dear Clara,
He could not make more charming than it is,
So I perceive he has not flattered *you* ;
Nor is his Juliet, which you've hanging here,

One whit more fair than the original.
Have you e'er seen his sister ? I suppose
You know the face is hers ?"

       " I knew it not,"
Replied the Lady Clara. " Save by you,
I am not certain that I ever heard
His sister named ; but I remember this—
Not long ago my brother said to me,
When standing by me, gazing on the picture,
' Clara, you often ask when I will marry ;
Find me a face like *that*, and I will wed.' "

 " Indeed !" exclaimed the Marchioness ; " 'tis strange
He should not have discovered whose it was.
Goes he not oft to Grantley's studio ?"

 " Sometimes," responded Clara, " once with me ;
But of Miss Grantley nought we saw or heard,
Nor was she mentioned by her brother here."

 " Too proud, perhaps, he was to speak of her,"
Replied the Marchioness ; " he might have thought
The naming her were hint she might be asked
To Castle Valmont during his own stay ;
And *that* your mother, whose punctilious dread
Of all plebeian contact you well know,
Would never take. It seems that you, my dear,
Were far too civil in her rigid eye

          3—2

To Grantley, tempting him to gaze on you
Too freely, and I gather that he left
In something like a huff, because she said so.
Now if, in copying your charming face,
He'd used soft speeches, umbrage had been due;
But *looks* it is the artist's privilege
To use by beauty's side, without restraint.
But here's the Earl; shall we enlighten him?
Valmont," she cried aloud, as he approached,
" I've news for you.   Prepare to pay your vows,
Or be accounted traitor to your word;
Who said with such a sentimental sigh—
' Show me a face like that and I will marry;'
What if I tell you where it may be seen?"

    The Earl looked vexed, but wishing to escape
The banter of the Marchioness, replied—
" Clara shall tell me, for I see she knows,
Meantime you'll find amusement on the lawn.
I'm sent to say there's archery in play,
Or, if you fancy more exciting sport,
Bludgeons and pipes are flying fast about
Aunt Sally's sable skull—with small success—
For my fair friends, who've turned so many heads
Without attempting, cannot now turn one,
Striving with all their might."

                        " Attempt or not,
They've failed with you, my lord; but who shall say

Transferred to canvas what they might not do ?
But I am gone, I see you grow impatient,"
Said the gay Marchioness, and flew away.

" Now, Clara," said the Earl, when she was gone,
" What made you give the Marchioness my words
About that picture ?   When I uttered them
I little dreamed what I have since discovered,
That Juliet's Grantley's sister ; I have seen her,
So no more jesting with the Marchioness
On what I said.   What's passed 'twixt you and
     her ?
You do not look as you were much surprised ;
My news, perhaps, has been forestalled by her ? "
Clara confessed it had, and then repeated
All from the Marchioness that she had heard.

" Clara," said Valmont, after she had ceased ;
" In speaking of my interview with Grantley,
I told you *all* that passed 'twixt me and him
Was not for you to hear ; therefore, withheld
What you've since learnt, till I had pondered well
My future course.   I have determined it :
If I shall find the manners and the mind
Accordant with the face I now have seen,
Its owner, will she, shall be Countess Valmont.
Now that the form, on which my thoughts have fed,
Has flashed in living beauty on my sight,
What was but once a dream, has grown a hope ;

What but a vision, playing round my brain,
A radiant reality, that pours
Its beams into my heart.   Yes, I have seen her:
She came before me like an angel visitant,
To smile and vanish; yet stayed long enough
To wake in me the instantaneous wish
To clasp her as my own, and blend at once
Her destiny with mine.   She nothing knows
Of what I feel; 'twas but by accident
That I had sight of her—as she came in
To Grantley, deeming he had been alone,
With courteous gesture, and a word to him,
Withdrawing, when she saw me.   In the mood
Grantley then was, I did not care to press
For introduction; and 'tis now my wish
To see her, if 't be possible, without
His intervention.   How that may be done
I mean to ask the Marchioness; she's heard
So much, 'twere better now to tell her more,
And win, by giving her my confidence,
Her silence and her friendship.   She, no doubt,
Can tell me much I might not learn elsewhere,
And help me, from her knowledge of Miss Grantley,
To shape my course in most befitting way
To win her heart and hand.   Till won they be,
Keep secret my design; I stay not now
To ask your thoughts of it, for I must seek
The Marchioness at once, ere she has time
To echo what you've told her to our guests."

Reply was starting quick to Clara's lips,
But Valmont broke too hurriedly away,
And soon was thus addressing her he'd sought—
"A word with you, dear Marchioness : don't laugh,
For really I'm as serious as I look.
You said just now, ' Prepare to pay your vows,
Or be accounted traitor to your word.'
I mean to pay them, for I feel I am
Far gone as Romeo's self ; so far, indeed,
That though, perchance, I shall not go the length
Of killing others first, and then myself,
In honour of *my* Juliet, I'm resolved
To conquer all obstructions that come not
From her own will.   To drop all metaphor,
I mean to win Miss Grantley, if I can,
And in my wooing may invoke your aid.
But, though they say no loving man is wise,
I'm not quite so *entêté* as to spurn,
Because she's fair, more knowledge than I've gained
From but a momentary sight of her—
Of the true self that 'neath her beauty lives.
The lady and her brother both, it seems,
Are known to you.   To me the latter is,
Of course ; and you will ask me, why from him
I do not seek all I desire to learn.
There are good reasons why ; let that suffice.
But good or ill, inform me what you know,
Frankly, and with no aim that what you say
Should spur me to, or drive me from, my suit."

" I see, my lord," replied the Marchioness,
" Ere you engage her services for life,
You'd have from me your helpmate's character.
Well, I can give you good report of her,
For, waiving all objection on the score
Of birth, connection, and that sort of thing,
She is a woman who, were I a man,
Would take my fancy more than any belle
Within Belgravia's sphere.   I won't describe
A face you've seen : her manners, full of grace
And gentle cheerfulness, have a reserve
That rises into dignity beside
The freer habitudes of those who join
In fashion's licensed levities ; her mind
Is rich and pure, and oft its culture shows
In thoughtful words, that shame the brainless chatter
Which passes current in our social groups
For conversation.   Of accomplishments
I can enumerate a goodly list :
She reads and speaks Italian, German, French,
Knows her own language, too, and reads in that
Books which at ' Mudie's ' meet with small demand,
At least from readers of our own sweet sex.
Sketches with skill, piano plays and harp,
And sings with taste ; in short, she only wants
A sprinkle of the sciences and classics
To fit her for a competent instructress
Unto those hopeful bairns in whose behalf
Paterfamilias offers, in the *Times*,

Kind treatment in a pious family,
And thirty pounds per annum.   There, my lord,
Has what I've said put wings upon your heart,
Or made it heavier for its destined flight,
If 'tis not flown already ?   But explain
In what way I can aid you in your suit ?
Wherein lies the impediment, if you
Have made a conquest of your pride ? "

                              " *Her* pride,"
Replied the Earl ; " a pride which seems to me
To go beyond, or rather overfly,
My mother's or my own.   I can perceive
In what you've told me, and still more from what
I've gathered from her brother, that my rank
Will rather hinder than advance a suit
Your words make me more eager to pursue.
Say ; can you help me to an interview
Where I might meet her as if undesigned ?
She's fond of music—you've an opera box ;
Might I not there have speech with her ? "

                              " I'll think,"
Replied the Marchioness, " of what you say.
She's very proud, I know ; 'twas long before
My friendliest overtures could meet response.
She very frankly told me that she thought
All rank contemptuous, haughty, insincere,
To all without its pale, save those whose wealth

Could give requital for its condescension.
I can't make out that she has ever loved,
But offers more than one she has refused
From wealthy suitors.   I remember once
It was an evening's gossip at Torlonia's,
Of three admirers which would win her hand ;
And when I told her of the talk, she said—
' When the choice lies 'twixt dotard, boy, and fool,
Methinks, dear Marchioness, the candidates
Might seek election at some lady's hands
Whose fingers itch a little more for gold
Than mine do yet.'   But mostly when I spoke
Of marriage, she would cut me short with this—
' When'er I wed, I wed a gentleman ; '
Dilating sometimes in such words as these :
' Equality must be our bond in all ;
In love, in years, in manners, and in mind."
And if I added, ' station,' she would say—
' Wait till it tempt me ; wedded I for rank,
'Twould be but rising in the social scale
By sinking in the moral.   If from that
Must come a husband, let me die a maid.'
So now you have some clue to her ideas,
You'll find, perchance, the key to her affections.
If I can help you, you may count on me ;
But break off now, I have a score of bets
Upon the archery ; when that is o'er
We'll talk again, and, meantime, trust to me
For secresy and silence."

PART IV.

'Twas now that so called " season " of the year
When 'tis the wont of England's wealth and rank
To flock to London, thronging its full streets
To pay their annual worship to the gods
Of fashion's temple—gathered there to play
Each his own great or little part upon
The grandest stage civilization boasts ;
A jumble strange of actors, high and low,
Moving about in a commingled scene
Of pleasure, pride, ambition, vanity,
Patrons of aught that ministers to these,
Whether the artist be buffoon or sage
That proffers them his service ; till the quacks,
Who block up merit's many thoroughfares
Around this swelling city's " mighty heart,"
Leave small room for the few realities
That venture in the push for precedence.
To their town mansion had the Valmonts come,
But, ere arrival, to his sister's ear
The Earl confided all that he had learnt

Touching the Grantleys—of their early life
And education 'neath their uncle's roof,
With other matters which, on further talk
From time to time, the Marchioness disclosed.
The Lady Clara listened patiently,
And said no word against his cherished hopes,
For she well knew that Valmont had a will
Which brooked no opposition when once formed.
But she foresaw collision must arise
Betwixt him and their mother, when she came
To hear of his attachment ; and as much
She said to Valmont ; but his curt reply
Was—" When it haps, I shall know how to meet it."

They had not from the country long returned
When from the Marchioness arrived this note—
" Miss Grantley, who's my guest for a few days,
To-night goes with me to the opera."
" Clara," said Valmont, after he had read it,
" I *shall* go to the opera to-night."

In Flotow's " Martha " is a touching air
Which sweetly falls on every listening ear,
But falls on none so sweetly as the lover's
In presence of his mistress.   To this air
Valmont was listening as, beneath the box,
Where she was seated, he perceived Lucille
Wrapped in the music also ; as he gazed,
Their glances met, and ere the plaudits closed

That followed on the song, he stood beside her.
Some formal words of recognition over,
And after talk of Mario's charming voice,
Flotow's weak music, Valmont, smiling, said,
" Miss Grantley, are you grieving not to find
Some drapery here 'neath which you might escape
And vanish from my presence, as you did
So quick when first we met ? "

                              " My lord," replied she,
" My brother's studio was not quite the place
For me, in presence of his lordly patron.
The Marchioness is kind enough to say
Her friends are mine, at least while I am with her ;
But were they not, I should not stand in fear
Of aught that made me anxious for *escape*,
Or feel their company so overwhelming
That their withdrawal would be my relief ;
Tho' mine, perchance, were theirs."

                              " My dear," broke in
The Marchioness, " you're cynical to-night.
You can't suppose Lord Valmont so absurd
As to believe his presence really awed
One like Miss Grantley ; he but hinted that
It might not be so welcome as he wished."

    Valmont drew back, but looked so earnestly
Into Lucille's already softening eye,

As if to read the soul that slept beneath,
That his own secret flashed into clear light;
Flashed for a moment, as the shrouded moon
Lies all exposed beneath some sudden gust
Of searching wind, then hides itself again
To beam no more till earth withdraws its frown.
But for a moment,—yet it was enough
To tell the shining secret of his soul;
Shining more clearly for the dark surroundings
From which it stole, as if despite itself.
No revelation was it to despise,
Still less to doubt; for faith it seemed to ask,
And *that*, at least, deserved.

      The Marchioness
Had turned, and kept her eye still towards the stage,
After those few words to Lucille, nearer whose side
Valmont, unfixing his more serious gaze,
Now drew, and, bending o'er her, gently said—
"Miss Grantley, if I've given you offence,
My tongue has wronged me, but you've wronged me more
In arming yours with such a bitter edge.
The Marchioness has asked me to her house
To-morrow night; she says you will be there,
And being sure of that, makes sure of me,
But if my absence—why, I will not ask—
Will be an element, however small,
In adding to the pleasure you may find
From others' company, say frankly so,
And mine shall not there fret you, or elsewhere."

" My lord," replied Lucille, " your grave rebuke
Would make me smile but that I see *'tis* grave.
Cutting and bitter words are sometimes said
Without intention, and the speaker wound
More than the hearer.   Well, I promise you
That if we meet again to-morrow night,
My voice shall sound less harshly ; I'm to sing,
As probably you know."

　　　　　Of some reply
Valmont was thinking, when the curtain fell ;
The Marchioness rose, asking for her shawl ;
Lucille already had adjusted hers.
They leave the box, and soon are in the crush,
Not by the Marchioness borne so patiently
As by Lucille, whose hold of Valmont's arm
Had driven all other contact from her thoughts,
And brought her, dreaming, to the carriage-steps,
Scarce then awake till he had said " Good-night."

" My dear, what made you," said the Marchioness,
After the carriage was well on its way,
" Repel so rudely Grantley's best of friends,
And not the worst of mine ?   I little thought
Such bitterness was in you, all this time,
About that matter with the Lady Clara."

Replied Lucille, " Did I *so* bitter seem ?
Indeed, I should not more respect myself,

Or hope, by others, to be more respected
For bitter feelings, or for bitter words :
But my great struggle is this hate of rank—
Turning its nose up at humanity
In want of wealth or pedigree, and leagued
To ostracize from its well-fenced domains
Whoever ventures to seek entrance there,
Without credentials from that motley court
O'er which great Garter King-at-Arms presides.

   " There, there, Lucille, no more of all this stuff ! "
Exclaimed the Marchioness, " or you'll go mad ;
Child—for you're one with all your years and wisdom—
Do you not see that this same gentleman
Whom we'll *not* call Earl Valmont, if it riles you,
Loves you, and fain would win you, if he can ?
Now tell me what's to hate in that—or him ? "

   " I hate him not," replied Lucille, " and yet—"

   " Yet what ? " rejoined the chafing Marchioness.
" If you do not, don't speak as if you did,
Listen with patience, if you can't with love,
And keep your scorn for—Garter King-at-Arms."

   No more was said before they were at home,
But ere they parted for the night, they talked
Again together, and in such a strain
As made the Marchioness write Valmont thus—

"Be here to-morrow; I have probed her thoughts,
And find her seeming iciness but pride
Which only thinly surfaces her heart,
And soon will melt beneath love's genial breath.
But for the titled prefix to your name
'Twould melt at once—nay, e'en *with* that but for—
I use *her* words—' *your arrogant disdain
Of such alliances.*' Here let me say
Naught that *I've* hinted compromises *you*.
I put your preference but as my surmise;
To which she answered, ' 'twas impossible
That one whose sentiments were such as yours
Would stoop to marriage with a tradesman's daughter.'
This is the thorn that rankles in her heart,
And you alone have power to pluck it forth.
That she loves you, I would not dare to say,
That you love her, she will not dare believe;
Had she such credence, if I read her rightly,
Her heart is yours, but I am half asleep,
And my poor maid is quite; so now—*bon soir.*"

Next evening came, and to the Marchioness
An early guest came Valmont; he had had
Words with his mother, which had made him deem
She half suspected all his sister knew;
The words had chafed him, but had shaken not
His now established purpose. With a smile—
Not that mere simper ever at command,
But that sweet radiance of a woman's eye,

4

Which is more kind than warm, more warm than bright,
And, less from courtesy than feeling sprung,
Beams with the sunshine of her own true heart ?—
For true I hold it, mainly, to be found
All the world o'er, spite the flawed glass which shows
It otherwise, and spite the Fall's sad tale,
Which ne'er has made me waver in the faith
That from Eve came humanity's best half.
But whither am I wandering ?—

                  With a smile
Of meaning, then, that makes the word no lie,
Lucille accepted Valmont's proffered hand,
And freely conversed with him, till she rose
To move to the piano, where her harp
Was waiting for her hand in a duet.
Valmont stood by her for the first few notes,
And then retreating through the gathering crowd
Of circling listeners, stood apart to hear,
Or rather, watch her, as she swept the strings
With most caressing touch ; revolving thus—
" What bliss it were, like her own instrument,
Unto that gentle bosom to be drawn,
And held there till each fibre of my heart
Thrilled, as those chords now thrill within her arms.
Mine she shall be, if there be wit in me
To win her, and that soon ; no more suspense ;
Tongues will be prattling if I tarry long,
In fashion I should brook not for *her* sake.
In what concerns it, or concerns it not,

The world has peering eyes ; and oft the spot
That should be sacred from its faintest glance
' Is penetrated with its insolent light.'
I can perceive from sundry glances here,
'Tis growing curious on *my* account ;
There shall not long be mystery between us ! "

     Thus Valmont mused, as all alone he stood,
Watching Lucille, till in a reverie
So deep he grew enwrapped as scarce to mark
The closing of the music, until she,
Passing herself, escorted to her seat,
Made him aware that she had ceased to play.
Roused from the current of his thoughts, he moved
To where she sat, and bending o'er her said—
" Music, Miss Grantley, always sets me dreaming.
'Tis Moore, I think, who tells us it ' can touch
Beyond *all else* the soul that loves it much.'
I know of one thing that can touch it more."
     " Than music—what ? " Lucille looked up and said.
     He answered quick, " When *you* play—the *musician*."

     With a slight flush she turned her face away,
Murmuring some words that reached not the Earl's ear.
For at that moment Lady Valmont's name
Was called aloud, and ere he could break through
The crowd to join her, she was by his side,
Gazing where she could recognize at once
Miss Grantley ; 'twas the first time they had met,

                                                  4 -- 2

But Juliet now was known as Grantley's sister,
And there she sat with all of Juliet's charms,
As in the picture " which had so bewitched,"
For so she termed it—" her demented son."

 " Mother," cried Valmont, " what has brought you here ?
I thought you said the Marchioness had grown
Too miscellaneous in her guests for *you ?*
Where's Clara ?"
                " Mind not her, 'tis you I seek,"
Answered the Countess,—" *that* has brought me here,
Though 'tis no place for either ; half this mob
Are strangers to us both, and ought to be,
Altho' I see Miss Grantley *is* among them ;
Pray don't abandon her on my account,
But when your flirting's over, we will go."

 Valmont said naught, but seized his mother's arm,
And, chafing, almost swung her from the room,
Scarcely less quickly hurried her downstairs
Into her carriage, and exclaiming, " Home ! "
In tone that startled her, no other word
Deigned till he stood within that home again.

 " Valmont," the Countess said, when they'd alighted,
" Let's understand each other ; if you are
So blind, so weak, so foolish, or so mad
As to pursue with any serious thoughts
This artful girl, who, at the best, is but

A pretty model for a painter's brush,
Say so, that I may put you on your guard,
And tell you plainly, you'd disgrace your name
Far less by making her your concubine
Than wife."
        Rage—indignation—shame—
To hear such words come from his mother's lips
Kept Valmont still as silent as before ;
At length he spoke—
            " Mother, till now I've borne
With your imperious nature as a son
Alone could bear ; your wishes have obeyed
In all things where obedience seemed not sin,
That discord ne'er might rise between our hearts ;
You've ever had my love ; you have it still ;
But look not for my reverence again
If you would urge me marriage to forego
With any virtuous woman that I love,
Tho' she were but a peasant in the fields—
Instead of what Miss Grantley is, a lady—
For such an infamous alternative
As you have dared to hint to me just now.
I love Miss Grantley ; tho' I've yet to learn
That she loves me ; I'll win her if I can ;
I cannot help it if it wounds your pride ;
With eight and twenty years upon my head
I claim to be the master of my choice
In what shall make, or mar, my future life ;
It is not my fault that, within the sphere

To which my birth assigned me, I have found
No woman that e'er raised in me the wish
To make her the companion of such thoughts
As I keep for a wife. Nay—mother dear—
Be patient while I speak, and look not thus,
Although your son, I shall be firm in this—
Do no rash act, say no rash words that may
Sever us past reunion ; on my knees
I shall be praying soon that you may look
On my resolve more calmly ; on *your* knees
Pray that your son may do no viler act
Than wed the virtuous lady that he loves,
Nor leave a deeper stain upon his scutcheon
Than heir whose grandsire earned his bread by trade !
And now, Good night." He stooped to kiss her cheek,
As almost fearing she would wave him off ;
She did not, but would give him no return :
He said again, " Good night." No answer came ;
He took her hand, and pressed it ; " Mother dear—
Once more—Good night." She put away his hand,
But said, at length, " Good night "—and so they parted.

   And so they parted—in no mood for rest ;
Valmont, the parley with his mother passed,
Began to fear that his abrupt departure
Might to the Marchioness have caused offence,
And raised suspicion in Miss Grantley's mind
Of what his mother's manner scarce concealed.
Return he soon resolved, and in an hour

From time of his departure, he again
Stood listening to her music, and—yet sweeter—
To her voice also ; she was in the midst
Of a new ballad that was much in vogue,
Bearing for title its concluding strain—
" No, not with *thee !*"—the song itself ran thus :—

1.

Praising too much his gentle art,
The lady won the minstrel's heart;
He followed her o'er land and sea,
Where'er she wandered,—wandered he.

2.

She loved another all the while,
But lured him on with constant smile;
And e'er beside her did he roam,
Till both resought their native home.

3.

The lady found her loved one wed,
And to the minstrel came, and said—
"From this cold clime again I flee;
Wilt take thy harp, and follow me?"

4.

" What, that same harp," the minstrel cried,
" I struck so proudly by thy side ;
I fear its sweetest sounds are flown,
But listen whilst I try their tone."

5.

To hear again that well-known lyre,
Her eyes flashed forth their softest fire ;
But faint and fainter grew their ray,
As thus the minstrel sang his lay,

6.

"You call me hence to softer skies,
And thus my tempted heart replies—
'Oh! there what bliss once more to be;
But not with thee—no, not with *thee!*

7.

"The sunny scenes of that sweet clime,
Mid nature fair, and art sublime,
My prayer it is once more to see;
But not with thee—no, not with *thee!*'

8.

"Go, fickle mind, and falser heart,
To that fair clime, alone, depart
Where I would dwell—where I would flee;
But not with thee—no, not with *thee!*"

There was a murmur of applause as died
On Lucille's lips the words—"No, not with thee;"
But Valmont, as their mournful cadence fell
Upon his ear, half took them to himself;
And had no heart for compliment, although
Charmed, like the rest, by voice whose plaintive tone
With deepest meaning blended sweetest sound.
'Twas late before the company dispersed,
Allowing Valmont opportunity
For oft-repeated converse with Lucille.
He lingered long, and when she said, "Good night,"
As the first streaks of dawn began to show,
He said half smiling, "Were the night not gone,
I might reply, 'Parting is such sweet sorrow,
That I could say '—you know the rest—adieu."
And so *they* parted.

PART V.

A FÊTE CHAMPÊTRE—less picturesque, perchance,
Than may be read of in Boccaccio's page,
Or seen on Wattcau's canvas ; yet presenting
Features attractive to the painter's eye
If not the poet's : high above, nor far
From the proud city which it overlooks
At pleasing distance, stands a mansion fair,
From whose green slopes and terraced steps descend
Group after group in rich and gay attire,
Spreading themselves wherever chance or choice
Determines them to wander, in a scene
Where art and nature have combined their charm
With wond'rous witchery ; dispersing—some
Through statued avenues in trellised walks
Where flowers and fruits of choicest culture bloom ;
Some by the paths where falling fountains feed
The baths beneath that shine with golden fish ;
Some breaking off through groves and shrubberies
Into the wilder beauties, only reached
By careful footing they forget to take
Till laughter follows at their reckless haste :
Others seek out where mimic rock and dell

Promise seclusion, or where ear and eye
Find sweet employment in the sight and sound
Of gushing waters ; minstrels, here and there,
At intervals unlooked for music make,
Startling the listener with a sweet surprise.
From greenest lawn the target's rainbow-hues
Gleam thro' the trees to tempt the archer's skill—
In chosen spots goes merrily the dance ;
Some rest, some walk ; above, beneath, around,
All yielding to the joyance of the hour,
And basking 'neath a summer sky and sun
Blending Italian softness with the breath
Of winds that cling, like lovers, to the leaves ;
Stirring them only with a gentle thrill
Of tremulous delight.

                    So fair the day
And such the scene in which Lucille, at length,
Heard words that sent the blood into her cheek,
And palsied all her speech,—fond words poured forth
In the brief moments 'twixt the dance's close
And her reunion with the Marchioness,
By whose side now she sits.   What had she felt
That still she trembles, though the speaker's gone ?
Need it be told what every woman feels
Who listens to be told she is beloved,
And hears it from the lips of him who loves ?
How loth the proffered homage to reject,
E'en where rejection must be ; what kind care

To clothe refusal in its gentlest shape ;
Yet, when acceptance is the heart's reply,
Denial sometimes struggles from the lips,
And such denial had striven to leave Lucille's,
But striven in vain ; the prudence and the pride,
Of which she had to Eustace urged so much,
Now, that her own heart stood in need of guard,
Like treacherous sentinels had disappeared,
And left her powerless in the grasp of Love,
Powerless—or Valmont she had told at once
That bride of his she would not deign to be ;
Had given him for answer his own words—
" That Tradesmen's daughters were not mates for Peers : "
Had stung him, even as Eustace he had stung,
Paying him pride for pride, and scorn for scorn.
All this was in her thoughts when he at first
His love to tell, and how it rose, began ;
But as his words more tender, earnest, grew,
She felt there was a music in his voice
Which gave the echo of too true a heart
To shock or wound with virulent repulse ;
Repulse—to one who had breathed in her ear
The dearest words that man can speak to woman ?
To one on whom her sex's brightest smiles
Had shone in vain—whose talents, tastes, pursuits,
Lifted him higher than his rank or wealth,
One too the portrait of whose face and form
Had oft her silent admiration won
In Grantley's studio, fed on by her,

As hers had been by Valmont—repulse to him ?
The thought arose, but, sinking, rose no more ;
She heard him to the close, and when he ceased,
Ending with urgent, passionate appeal
That 'neath her own roof he might visit her,
And there repeat what then he had avowed,
In presence of her brother, she could give
No answer haughtier than this, that she
" Was too much taken by surprise to say,
What *then* might be—but would he leave her now ? "

The Marchioness, divining what had passed,
Felt no surprise, when Valmont had departed,
To hear Lucille of weariness complain ;
Nor, as her visit was to end that day,
At her request to go back home at once.

When there arrived she did not hesitate
To tell to Eustace all the Earl had said,
Revealing frankly her own feelings too,
But saying, as she ended the recital,
" Not what I would, but what I should, dear brother,
Help me to do."   To which he quick replied :
" No reason why you should not what you *would* ;
You love and are beloved ; had I been sure
Of Lady Clara's heart, I would have dared
To ask her hand ; I would not ask it now,
Nor ever shall—come what may of your love :
And therefore can with greater freedom give

Counsel to you.   The Earl's been my best friend ;
And tho' he spoke some cutting words to me,
In ignorance of how they might, one day,
Be turned against himself, still, if he woos
My sister as a gentleman should woo
A lady, let him win her if he can.
So, sister dear, his fate is in your hands ;
I think I see your heart, your judgment must
Decide the rest."
             Upon the morrow came
The Earl to Grantley, and thus frankly spoke :
" Grantley, you doubtless guess why I am here—
To ask your sanction to an interview
With that same lady whom, in Juliet's form,
My fancy made an idol of, until
Her own appeared, and to my fancy's flight
Added my heart's ; and now I come
To learn if it be possible to win
Her own heart in return ?"
             Then Eustace thus :
" My lord, remembering your former words,
I'm almost tempted to exclaim with Portia,
' Of a strange nature is the suit you follow ; '
But if the suit contents you, and you choose
To break, or leap, all barriers of your own
To win my sister, it must rest with her
To say if she will enter what remains
Forbidden ground to me.   This way, my lord.
Lucille," continued Eustace, as she rose

At Valmont's entrance, " 'tis his lordship's wish
To have some private converse with yourself;
With what design he has no secret made,
With what success I leave him now to learn."

" Miss Grantley," said the Earl, as Eustace left,
" Or may I drop this heart-belying phrase,
And say, ' Lucille ? ' " and nearer to her drawing,
He took her hand, exclaiming, " Dear Lucille !
I have already told you that I love you ;
And now I come to tell you that I feel
My happiness depends on your reply.
I know the answer I deserve to have ;
I saw it flash, like lightning from thine eye,
When yesterday I first revealed the hope
Repeated now ;—hope which had gone to wreck
But for the anchor of thy gentler heart,
Which held me fast amid thy stormier thoughts.
But to that anchor am I safely bound,
Or is its chord impatient of its strain ?
Because in holding me, it holds my rank.
No, you will never fling me off for that,
Which is no fault of mine, nor yet defect,
If there be naught unworthy in myself,
And 'tis myself I offer, not my rank,
Which, in thine eyes, I know, is valueless,
And in my own alone deserves respect
When he who wears it is respected too,
And grows to *be* the nobleman he's called.

Had I presumed upon my name and birth,
My daily life is where I find their spell
As potent as they here are powerless.
Were I in quest of beauty for a mate,
Need I have left where is my daily life ?
I've had my roaming fancies of the eye ;
But never, till that eye was fixed on thee,
Beheld the woman who could tempt my tongue
To speak to her of love ; into your ear
'Tis poured for the first time, perchance the last,
If you reject it ; sudden though it seem,
It is no passion's momentary gush,
No sensitive impulsion of a heart
That takes the warmth of every passing smile,
Or palpitates with every passing breath,
But the unfolding of a pent-up flower
Increasing in unconscious growth and strength,
And only waiting for its sun to rise
To burst beneath its light ; that sun art thou ;
And now thy answer ; tell me, may I give
To you the dear and sacred name of wife ? "

There was a pause, as if her breath had gone :
At length began Lucille with faltering voice—
Faltering at first, but soon becoming firm :
" Unclasp my hand that I may strive to say
What must be said before I answer give
Unto the solemn question you have put.
I would not be accused of reticence

In aught that you should know, but might not learn,
Till knowledge came too late ; in wedding me
You raise my humbler station to your own,
Though if I know myself, I do not doubt
To hold it as becomes Earl Valmont's wife ;
But change of sphere will work no change in *me* ;
My habits—tastes—attachments—principles—
Will still remain ; are you so well assured
That none of these may bring you shock or shame ?
What if my creed be one to which your Church
Assigns the epithet of infidel,
Though creed of Milton, Newton—of the sage
Who traced man's understanding to its source,
Of him who sang " Evangeline," and of her
In whose sweet strains so many infant lips
Hymn their first praise to God ?   This creed hold I,
And, true to me as yours is true to you,
Must hold without concealment or disguise.
Then I have kindred not to be renounced
By me, howe'er unwelcome to yourself ;
And first, my brother—he, where'er I dwell,
Must enter—not upon mere sufferance,
Or under guarantee of good behaviour,—
You smile, my lord ; but after what has passed
'Twixt him and you concerning Lady Clara,
'Twere well at once that I thus freely spoke ;
I might indeed, when once become your wife,
Insist, with sanction of both Church and State,
That all my kindred should be held your own,

Had I respect for any human code
To which instinctive Nature gives the lie ;
But still my kin, tho' then no more to you
Than now they are, will not be less to me ;
And such few friends as I and Eustace have
I would preserve ; my habits and my tastes
Might clash with yours : some things I've learnt to count
As daily duties, and, whate'er my rank,
Would still perform ; I could not live the life
Which titled ladies, for the most part, lead,
Or seem to lead from all I know or see,
Without a forfeiture of self-respect,
Without entire forgetfulness of Him
Who asks some worthier service at the hands
Of his most noble creatures, than a life
Of luxury or ease ; so ponder well,
My lord, before you take to your proud halls
One who is such as I've avowed myself,
And means to be no other."

              As she ceased,
Valmont resumed her unresisting hand,
And passionately pressing it, exclaimed—
" No other would I have thee ; in thy words—
Faithful to others, as thyself, I hear
The best assurance of thy faith to me
In all that gives fidelity its worth ;
The tie that makes thee mine shall leave thee free
Of every bond that thou wouldst spurn to wear ;

Walk as thou hast, teaching me how to rise
To the high standard of thy daily life,
A task, perchance, less hard than thou mightst deem,
For I have sense of deeper, purer needs
Than rank and wealth supply, and from the time
Which brought my steps to manhood's turning-point,
Have ever had an aim beyond the mark
Of those around me.   I have felt too much
The wickedness of unimproved existence
To tamely float down pleasure's lulling stream,
Or play the animal in human shape
Beneath civilization's cloak and mask ;
I would ennoble my humanity
By something higher than my name or birth,
And would, to be companioned in the effort
By head and heart like thine, forswear my rank,
Were needed such a sacrifice to win thee,
And leave ' my order ' to its own good care.
Take me for what I am, not what I'm called,
There is no need for pondering on your words.
Each has but fixed new rivets to my love ;
Let me go hence then with the sweet assurance
I have not loved—I do not woo in vain."

    So ending, to Lucille he nearer drew,
And, as his arm stole gently round her waist,
There was no shrinking from the coming clasp ;
From lips, not words, he took her answer now—
Parley was past, and silence was their joy.

PART VI.

WE left the Countess brooding o'er the shock
Of her son's free disclosure ; little sleep
Had she that night, and sullenly alone
Sat next day in her room, and hearing there
From Valmont of his offer to Miss Grantley,
So angry grew, that when he wrote to say
His hand had been accepted, she took up
Her pen and answered thus—" *We* meet no more."
Day after day he strove to soften her
By kindliest appealings, but in vain ;
In vain his sister spoke on his behalf,
And ventured something in Miss Grantley's praise.
The Countess, vowing " they were all conspirators,"
Would hear no word from any but her maid,
And, keeping to her bed-chamber, there sat
Denouncing Valmont, Clara, and, in words
Scarce fitting Christian lips, the Marchioness.
At times she'd murmur—" Is it really true ? "
And half persuade herself it could not be,
Valmont, her son, in web so vulgar caught,
For whom in vain love's finest, subtlest snares
Had oft been set !   What was Miss Grantley's charm ?

Virtue forsooth ! What *bait* was there in that ?
And beauty—was it nowhere to be found
But in the dressed-up jades who lent their looks
To make more saleable their brothers' daubs !
It must be stopped—what if she sought this girl
That looked at her so insolently calm
The other night, as if to say, " *He's mine,*
Tho' you *are* come."—What if she told her, Valmont,
Despite his promise, ne'er would marry her ?
'Twas a bold step, but something must be done
To shake her faith in him ere he could make
His word irrevocable by his acts.

    Revolving o'er and o'er these thoughts, one day
When Valmont was from London, she rose up,
And summoning her carriage, bid it drive
In a direction that would bring her near
To Grantley's residence, but stopping short of it
That none at home should of her visit learn.
'Twas her intention to attempt at first
Persuasion with his sister, ere she tried
The bolder course for which she came prepared ;
But the complacent air and tranquil mien
With which Miss Grantley bade her " take a chair "
Roused all her sleeping fury, and at once
With virulent abruptness, she broke out—
" My son, I find, is paying court to you,
And you allow it ; I presume you know
How courtship of such sort can only end :

You cannot think it possible that he
Will wed one so beneath him—do you hear ?''

   After a moment's pause came this reply—
" I do—but, madam, if you've more to say—
And wish me to be patient whilst I listen,
Find other terms to speak in ; nor so loud,
I am not deaf."

          " Indeed, but you are blind,"
Replied the still more chafing dowager,
" And somewhat insolent.   ' Find other terms ? '
And pray, Miss Grantley, what are they to be ?
Shall I be plain, and say, when love-sick maid
In station like your own consents to hear
The amorous talk of lover she must know
Can never be her husband,—'twere not strange
If she became his mistress ?''

              At that word
Lucille, as struck by an electric shock,
Sprung up with flushing brow and flashing eye,
And with indignant vehemence exclaimed—
"How dare you, madam, say such words to me ?
Tax *me* with insolence—this chamber's mine,
And I command you—leave it ; do *you* hear ?"

  " Miss Grantley," cried the Countess, half in rage
And half astonishment, but somewhat cowed

By the stern aspect and uplifted hand
Of the dilated form that o'er her stood,
Looking a deeper scorn than tongue could utter,
" Miss Grantley, pray sit down ; despite your wrath
I must say what I came for."

     " I'll not hear it,"
Was the quick ringing answer. " I cannot
Force you to leave my presence, but from yours
This door shall lock me if you'll not quit mine."

 Already was she moving to the portal
Which led to an adjoining room, her back
Turned on the Countess, who, then rising, spoke—
" You need not take the trouble to retire,
Don't make yourself a prisoner for me,
I came to give advice, not give or take
Offence ; but as you do not choose to hear,
The consequences be on your own head ;
Good day, Miss Grantley ! "

     "Home, quick, coachman, home !"
Were the sole words the Countess spoke for hours
After the scene depicted as above.
Next day and next, she took nor food, nor drink,
Till the physician by her bedside stood
And spoke of dangerous fever ; rapidly
It grew despite his care ; delirium came ;
Valmont and Clara were alike unknown
As they stood by her, listening to words

Which made her state more grievous to behold.
At length more tranquil she appeared to grow,
And might recover, the physician said,
But would require much watching, and much care,
So much of vigilance, indeed, said he,
That on her nurse her life might yet depend.

Valmont, who daily with Lucille conferred,
Had of his mother's visit heard from her,
But than that " angry words had passed 'twixt both,"
Could learn no more ; Lucille alarmed, distressed,
Began to urge him to forego her hand,
Or claim it not till time should reconcile
His mother to his choice—should she survive
Her present shock. Informed by Valmont now,
His mother's life might on her nurse depend,
She seemed a moment wrapped in earnest thought,
And then said quickly—" Let *me* be her nurse ;
I'm no Miss Nightingale, but I have had
Experience by the bedside of the poor
In my own neighbourhood, and know how much
The service of a gentle hand and voice—
Which I will give with all my heart and soul
To save your mother—can do for the sick."
The strange request took Valmont by surprise.
" What," he replied, " if she were to detect
You in her nurse ?—she has her lucid moments."
" Alas !" rejoined Lucille, " I know too well
She can't dislike me more than she does now ;

Besides I do not fear discovery,
I can, with little art, disguise my looks,
And, for my voice, she only knows it by
Tones she shall from it never hear again."

"I'll think of it," said Valmont, as he left,
"And with my sister will confer at once
How we may best receive you in our home,
Should our physician to your wish consent.
If you disguise yourself, as you propose,
None else need know you."

                  After his departure
She sat awhile reflecting on her scheme,
Praying that no rebellious pride might rise
In this new trial of her strength and will :
Thus fortified, she into Eustace went,
Who was in "Paul and Felix" still absorbed,
And told him of the service she had tendered.
"Do as you like," said he, "but don't submit
To any fresh indignity ; and mind,
The world will say all sorts of spiteful things ;
But you're not one to care for Mrs. Grundy
In aught you deem the right ; so kiss me, dear,
And go and be to others the good angel
You ever are to me."

              "I go disguised,"
Remarked Lucille, returning his fond kiss,
"Can you suggest how that may best be done ?"

Eustace looked well at her, and then exclaimed,
" Your eyebrows darkened, frontlet of black hair ;
Your cheeks embraced by a decorous cap,
Your hands unringed, your dress uncrinolined,
Will transformation so complete effect
That it would puzzle *me* to find you out."

" I go at once, then," said Lucille, " to try it."
And before night she'd everything prepared
To make the change ; before her glass she sat
Trying to tint her eyebrows, when a note
Was brought to her from Valmont, running thus—
" All is arranged ; be here at noon to-morrow,
We shall not send the carriage, lest it raise
Suspicion in our servants." With his note
Came kind one also from the Lady Clara,
Bidding her ask for her when she arrived.

Week followed week, and Lucille still remained
'Neath Valmont's roof, without discovery
By the sick Countess, who, thus gently tended,
Was growing slowly into calmer mood
Of mind and body ; latterly had shown
No symptom of delirium ; recognized
Valmont and Clara, and to their kind words
Had kindly answered ; but more kindly still
Talked with Lucille, who oft to her would read,
And sometimes soothe her into sleep with song ;
Thus one day when the Countess had expressed

A wish for something suited to the sick,
Lucille, as if from printed page reciting,
Ventured upon these verses of her own—

What though sickness lay us low
If we purer, kinder grow;
Is it not sweet chastisement,
Less from earth than heaven sent?
Boon for which our God to thank
More than gift of wealth or rank,
Though these brought us mind and frame
To which suffering never came?

What though sick in heart and head
O'er some cherished vision fled,
If in place of it there spring
Others that can ne'er take wing;
Visions, in whose lovely light
Forms that did us once affright;
Foremost mid them Right and Duty—
Now attract us by their beauty?

Thus in sickness shapes arise
Health discerns not, or denies;
Angels who, when once the heart
Has received them, ne'er depart;
But like statues calm and solemn,
Each from its appointed column
In the temple of the soul,
Ever more the heart control.

" Read them again," the Countess, musing, said;
" Who is the author?" Lucille read again,
But answered not the question, till again
'Twas asked, and then with hesitating voice
Confessed the truth.

" Indeed," the Countess said,
" Show me the lines ; the handwriting yours too ?
And play and sing ? why, how came you a nurse ? "

Lucille a moment paused, and then replied—
" It is not my vocation, but I learnt,
In tending the sick poor, the rich as well
Might stand in need of gentler ministry
Than hired hands always give : so being told
A lady in this house was lying ill,
Whose life depended on a watchful nurse,
I tendered my own services, and thus
You see me here, not from necessity,
But choice."

" Strange choice ; what, then, *is* your vocation,
If I'm to call your service charity ? "

" I've none," replied Lucille, " that has a name,
Save finding such employment for my days
As shall some noble purpose give to life,
And leave no bitter memories in the hour
Of my departure from it ; I have means
That free me from the need of toil for bread,
The rental, scarcely, of an opera-box,
But yet enough for all my social wants,
And some few pleasures.   With my guardian died
What you would call *position*, but the lessons
He had implanted in my mind and heart

Remained, and went with me where'er I went;
Amid them, these most treasured of them all,
To turn each moment to its best account,
To take no step that carried me away
From self-denial, or from self-respect,
And ne'er to let false pride stand in the way
Of a kind action or a truthful word.
But for such lessons I had not been here,
For, though I do not shrink to enter them,
Sick chambers are not suited to my taste."

" Nor," said the Countess, kindly, " to your strength,
If I may judge from that pale countenance ;
You must have found me very troublesome,
And not so patient as I mean to be :
Sickness is no bad teacher, as you say ;
And so you wrote those verses—hints to *me ?*
You need not speak, I know it by your look ;
I have been saying, I suppose, strange things ;
Have I been talking of Miss Grantley much ?
I mean the lady that's to wed my son,
If 'tis not done already ; tell me what
I said."

" You oft spoke bitter words of her,"
Replied Lucille, " but 'twas in your delirium,
You would not else have spoke *such* bitter words,
I'm sure, dear madam ! "

" How do you know that ?

Miss Grantley is a stranger quite to you,
And may have wronged me more than you imagine."

"But wrongs should be forgiven, should they not?"
Ventured Lucille.   "I know Miss Grantley well:
From her, indeed, I learnt the nurse's art;
And 'twas thro' her I came to wait on you.
She has been very wretched ever since
She heard of your sad illness, and I'm sure
Will never wed your son till you are well;
Nor then, perhaps, unless with your consent."

The Countess, with a searching look, exclaimed,
" Where did you get all this from?"   "From herself,"
Replied Lucille.   " She has been daily here,
Less to see Valmont than to hear of you."

The Countess started.   " Valmont, did you say?"
" I mean the Earl," said, flurriedly, Lucille.
But now the Countess suddenly sat up,
Placed her pale hand upon Lucille's flushed brow,
And, looking scrutinizingly in her face,
Said : " Woman, surely *you* are not Miss Grantley?"
Then adding quick, " My God, tho', but you are!"
Sank back, and for some minutes spoke no word.

Rising at length, she bid Lucille approach,
And after deeper survey, calmly said,
" I know those eyes; but that is not your hair;
And you are paler than when last we met,

And change complete has come upon your voice :
Or is it all disguise I see and hear ?
Tell me what's real and what's false in you."

   " There's nothing false in me," replied Lucille,
Taking off cap and braid, " but these, and they
Were for concealment, not deception, meant ;
In every office of my heart and hand
My real self has been by your bedside,
Through days and nights that have not wearied me
So much, but that 'tis still my hope to stay
Till you are quite recovered.   I *may* stay,
Dear madam, may I not ? "

                  The Countess paused,
Then said, composedly, " Yes, you may remain.
Why do you weep ?—come here—come here, and kiss
        me ! "
Lucille fell sobbing in the Countess' arms,
And felt the heaving of that haughty breast
Beat fondly 'gainst her own ; kiss after kiss
Came from those once harsh lips : the ice had burst
Of a proud nature 'neath the melting touch
Of one whose pride was greater, but whose love
Than that was greater still.

                  Thus lay these two
When Valmont entered.   From his mother's arms
Lucille then rose, Lucille without disguise.

In silent wonderment he gazed awhile
Till beckoned by the Countess to approach,
Who, taking his hand, placed it in Lucille's,
Saying, " My son, your choice is henceforth mine.
You shall be *both* my children when I'm well."

So ends my tale. What need to tell the rest ?
There was some talk about the *Earl's choice;* but
The tradesman's daughter, in the Countess Valmont,
Was soon forgotten : for a time it broke
The dull monotony of Rotten Row ;
But even the wheels of fashionable life
Rolled on without a stoppage,—almanacks,
Amid their most remarkable events,
Omitted this ; and although, when she died
Who once had been remembered as Miss Grantley,
The world had got some civil things to say,
There was small stir—save mid the many hearts
Which she had made the happier through her rank,
And in the halls to which she left an heir
Ennobled, as the Earl oft loved to say,
More by inheritance of his mother's nature
Than of his father's proud ancestral name.

I said my tale was ended, but a word
Is due to Eustace and the Lady Clara.
Of her, perchance, 'twill be enough to say
She ne'er was asked to be the wife of Grantley.
His life and heart were in his studio,

Where often high-born dames and damsels came,
From whom he sometimes most sweet glances had
Which he was too decorous to perceive,
Except upon his canvas to depict them.
He died—prosaic word—a bachelor—
But did not live a quite prosaic life,
If we may guess from sundry scraps of verse
From his own pen, amidst his papers found,
After his death—amid the rest were these :—

My fallen hopes! my fallen hopes!
    A sad adieu to ye,
And thou, beneath whose smile they rose,
    A sad adieu to thee!
Like leaves upon the moaning boughs
    Of summer's radiance reft,
That drop and drop, till on their stem
    No single one is left,
My fallen hopes! my fallen hopes!
    Ye thus have sunk away;
Till on this withered heart of mine
    There is not one to stay.

Yet as on earth's most barren spots
    Some flowers find soil to bloom,
And clinging to the rock are found,
    Or growing on the tomb;
The teeming thoughts within my brain,
    With sunny strength still rife,
Shall, flashing round my heart, awake
    Fresh blossoms into life.
Fresh blossoms—though from searching eyes
    They strive to hide in vain,
That others flourished once beneath
    Which ne'er will bloom again.

To thee, my own beloved Art,
  I turn for solace now ;
Farewell once more my fallen hopes,
  But ever welcome thou !
Chase the dark shadow from my breast
  With visions fair and bright,
Nor go from me till I have brought
  Their beauty into light ;
That after ages naming me,
  When *her* name is unknown,
May say, " Though in its tomb his heart,
  His mind was on its throne."

At Naples—1830.

I.

'Tis midnight—moonlight ! on the silent deep,
Within the sentried Lazaretto's view,
Moored beneath Nisida's o'erhanging steep,
Our bark at anchor lies ; to rest its crew
Are gone ; and I, ere this, had slumbered too,
But that the tranquil beauty of the night
Hath wakened thoughts which I would fain pursue,
E'en to the dawning of the morning's light,
Rather than close mine eyes upon so fair a sight.

II.

In such a scene how pure the heart's emotion,
Yon shore the eye might fancy Eden's own
When, side by side, in slumber or devotion,
Sleep hushed the breath, or prayer subdued the tone
Of earth's first pair embosomed there alone.
And ocean too—how mute and moveless, save
Where, flashing bright, some distant oar is shown,
Disturbing, only to illume, the wave,
As shall the seraph's hand that opes the good man's
    grave.

6—2

III.

'Tis morn, and rising round me I behold
Fresh beauty wake to life ; the swelling sea
In dyes of ever-varying hue unrolled
Like a rich carpet flashes gorgeously ;
On shore, the orange shines from many a tree,
'Bove which the festooned vines attract the sight,
Whilst 'neath the shadow of their drapery
Some terraced statue, catching the sun's light,
Strikes on the ravished eye from off its distant height.

IV.

Our anchor up, released from quarantine
To Nisida we gladly bid adieu !
No more obstructing islands intervene
To veil the shore, where Naples shines, from view :
Vesuvius greets us with its sombre hue,
Looking so tranquil we can scarcely deem
The tales of her volcanic vengeance true ;
So are not human spirits what they seem—
Oft in the softest eye lurks passion's fiercest beam.

V.

On, on we sail, till we can faintly hear,
As fast we glide along its foamless bay,
The murmurs of the city we draw near—
And over which the sun with tender ray,

More tender still, as drawing to decay,
Smiles lovingly, till brightening ere he die
He looks his last ; whilst as he sinks away,
Bathed in his beam, shore, city, sea, and sky,
In one commingling glow of roseate brilliance lie.

VI.

We land—I haste through crowded streets and squares.
Where to the stranger things *most* strange appear,
Polichinello, beggars, priests, screams, prayers,
Are all at first that catch his eye or ear ;
And well such sights and sounds may raise his sneer :
But soon it changes to a smile—for mirth
With superstition blends so quaintly here,
And to such freaks their union doth give birth,
Scarce wisdom's self could chide this merriest spot of
    earth.

VII.

Along the shore of Mergelline I roam,
To what doth yonder urchin beckon me ?
I quit awhile the beach of tideless foam
To follow him ; a steep acclivity
Above the town keeps winding gradually
To a wild garden's height ; I gaze no more
On palace, city, mountain, sky, or sea,
Intent on naught but what I stand before—
Words which the urchin shows o'er that wild garden's
    door.

VIII.

'Tis opened; 'neath a canopy of vines,
Whose fruit-pluck'd leaves still yield autumnal bloom,
By path that now ascends, and now declines,
I find the portal's promise—Virgil's tomb;
That such it is we may to doubt presume
Without heretic sin; though men have died,
Been cursed and threatened with perdition's doom,
For doubt of truths less clear; and still tongue-tied,
On points of creed-fenced faiths 'twere safer to abide.

IX.

I wander on until my steps intrude
On stones which bore the Cæsars' chariot wheel:
Part of the Appian way—fit spot to brood
O'er empire's emptiness—fit spot to feel
The truths, which 'tis time's mission to reveal:
Hovels are on the ground, rags in the air,
Where once triumphal arch, banner and steel
Glittered and waved—whilst they who now dwell there
Small trace of Roman soul or Roman aspect bear.

X.

Beggars and thieves acting the showman's part
Conduct my steps where oft the captive slave
Was brought to die, or learn the slaughterer's art;
Where oft was heard the lion's startling rave,

Or groan the dying gladiator gave
Beneath his fangs ; life cut most foully short
By death most ignominiously brave.
Why did not man and beast on man retort
And shed *his* blood who came to make *their* blood his
    sport ?

XI.

Who that beholds the briars o'er them spreading
Would wish again the circus walls complete,
Or sigh to see the goat and goatherd treading
Where man once lay beneath the tiger's feet ?
Oh, shame, that woman should e'er choose her seat
Amid such scenes, nor blush to keep her place !
That the death-thrust should its approval meet
In beauty's waving hand and smiling face,
Decked as if she had come some festal rite to grace.

XII.

The sun goes down upon the Baian bay,
Leaving the waters of its odorous shore
With breast still warm from the departing day ;
The breeze which on its wing sweet perfume bore,
Faint with its weight, has sunk and breathes no more :
Darkness steals like a lover on the light
Voluptuously sleeping ; not an oar
Ripples the wave ; silence is in her might,
Holding in charmed suspense the pausing step of night.

XIII.

Mid such a scene how oft must have reclined
Within his palace, which o'erlooked it all,
The tyrant Nero—could even *he* be blind
To beauty which might basest souls enthrall ?
Could it be *here* was heard the sleek foot-fall
Of the imperial monster when his slaves
Approached, obedient to his murderous call,
To hear the mandate for the deed which dyed
  Their hands in blood that stamped their master matri-
    cide ?

XIV.

Ah me ! that midst the fairest scenes which God
Unfolds to man such evil could be done.
To think, alas, what bloody steps have trod
Wherever shines Italia's gentle sun !
How few the spots where trace of them is none.
What tho' no Pagan temples mock its skies,
If deeds be wrought the Pagan's self would shun ?
Degraded Italy ! Yet who denies
  That 'neath thy soil the dust of many great men lies ?

XV.

Here Tasso dwelt ; we know how sad his lot,
Condemned in " prisoned solitude " to string
His harp's divinest chords ; yet failed he not
In strength or will. Imagination's wing

Took loftier flight, and showed how free could sing
The bard whose heart a princess held in thrall—
A thrall from which his deepest woe did spring,
For there were those who did it madness call—
The answer to that lie is in Ferrara's wall.*

XVI.

Yes—with the sound of the true maniac's chains
Clanking around him, did he burst his shroud
Of deadening grief, and break forth in such strains
As well might make the haughtiest princess proud
To own his love.   Dispelling every cloud,
Which, for the moment, had his mind o'ercast,
He woke his harp, which, ringing clear and loud,
Told to the world its transient blight had passed,
In tones that every age, which hears them, shall outlast.

XVII.

Revenge most fitting 'twas for him to take—
Leaving the blot which calumny would have thrown
Upon the mind oppression could not shake,
To spread its shadow o'er the oppressor's own—
A flame he raised to make that darkness known,
Which, in its immortality of shame,
The light it circled left more brightly shown—
'Tis thus that Genius dims its slanderer's name,
Fixing within its shade the blaze of her own fame.

* The MSS. of *Jerusalem Delivered* preserved in the prison
of Ferrara.

XVIII.

Evening again !—How touching is its close,
As if its light were being charmed away,
'Tis beauty when most beauteous—in repose.
The wind, which has been kissing earth all day,
Has ta'en at last its loving lips away,
And on the water's bosom sunk to sleep ;
The mountain shadows steal along the bay,
The flowers within their foliage seem to creep,
Till darkness hushes all in slumber soft and deep.

XIX.

Hark ! like the plaint of an imprisoned friend,
Mournful, but mighty and defying still,
Vesuvius hoarsely moans as we ascend.
Howl, demon, howl !   Although I feel a thrill
Within my breast which bodes my footsteps ill.
Again ! and see where, struggling thro' the dark,
From out the cavern he is doom'd to fill
His sulphury eyes their hollow circle mark,
Whilst e'er his rumbling throat keeps muttering ven-
        geance—hark !

XX.

Pompeii ! mute and melancholy ghost
Of life and light—funereal solitude !
Thou wilderness of walls without a host
To look from one !   City of death unviewed,

Untrod for centuries !   Dare I intrude
On thy sepulchral ground whilst still before thee
Thy fell consumer rages unsubdued,
Mighty as when he hurled destruction o'er thee,
And threatening even those who in thy tomb explore
    thee ?

XXI.

Doomed city—struck to that sepulchral mound
Which wrapped thy dead and living in one grave !
What ghastly relics of thy slain were found
When light and air showed what they could not save !
I see thy fall : the timid and the brave—
The sick—the hale—beauty—and those just blest
By beauty's smile.   Hark to their maniac rave !
They fly—they shriek—they pray—beat brain and
    breast,
" Down ! " the volcano roars—their murmurs are at rest !

XXII.

Yet see ! still struggling with the smothering ashes,
A thousand arms break desperately through ;
In vain ! with ceaseless and o'erwhelming crashes
The mountain doth his fiery bolts renew !
The air is choked—blotted the sky from view ;
With blinding fierceness, and light-blasting hue,
Clouds of red stones, and whirlwinds of black sand
O'er the doomed city hang—fall, hiss, expand—
Till all is hot and dark as Eblis's own land.

XXIII.

So fell Pompeii ! whilst her ashes lay
For eighteen centuries to man unknown,
Behold her now, unbosomed to the day,
Deserted, silent, but not yet o'erthrown :
Scarce from her streets is gone a single stone ;
The wheel is wither'd, but its track remains ;
Her walls are roofless, but there still unflown
The artist's colours glow ; though rent, her fanes
Yet standing are—and stand, as proud of their remains !

XXIV.

A day of storm ! the winds are on their wings,
And fiercely chase along the clotted air
The sulphur-breathing clouds ; the wave up-springs,
Lashed from its bed—and, as if in despair
Of ever undisturbed remaining there,
Rushes for refuge madly to the shore,
Only a fate more maddening still to bear :
Sternly the rocks repulse it o'er and o'er,
And strike the moaner back amid the ocean's roar.

XXV.

Thus are the wretched met when they would fly
The world's distraction : thus is fancy's dream
Of love and peace by life's reality
Broken and banished ; then comes reason's gleam,

Shining all cold and sad, like evening's beam,
Brightening the earth to leave it—a pale guide
To lonely paths—a beacon to redeem
The mind's lost track—too late! the averted tide
Of thought still darkly strays, till death its course doth
    hide.

XXVI.

Howl on, thou blast! I love thy raving shout,—
Thy wandering moan. Ye lightnings flash again!
Thus do my own o'erclouded thoughts rush out
With an electric frenzy from my brain
For mastery over darkness ; but in vain !
Even as, when your convulsive gleam is flown,
Naught but the gloomy thunder doth remain ;
The dirge-like echoes of my grief alone
Answer my spirit's burst with all-appalling tone.

XXVII.

What thoughts are these ? with faith in One above,
Is the spring clear whence such repinings flow ?
No more of them ! with Nature still to love
Who talks of an unconquerable woe ?
Where is the heart that feels not holier glow
And deeper joy in communing with *Her*,
Than passion in its purest hour can know ?
A love it is no selfish throb doth stir,
Whilst unto it all good and fair things minister.

XXVIII.

The love it is of every shifting scene
The seasons in their varied beauty show,
Of wind and wave, or stormy or serene,
Of leaves when green, or in their autumn glow,
When the boughs bend beneath the wintry snow,
Or the warm light through summer's foliage gleams ;
Where torrents roar, or streamlets gently flow ;
When morn is radiant, or 'neath moonlight beams,
When all those feelings wake the world calls idle dreams.

XXIX.

A love it is which makes it sweet to stand
Watching the waters on the lone sea-shore,
And feel the solitary heart expand
In the fond want of something to adore,
Though we be loved and thought upon no more ;
Till rises in each moaning of the wave
A sigh as 'twere *our* sorrows to deplore,
Whilst the tired waters, sinking where they lave,
Proclaim how earthly trouble ends but with the grave.

XXX.

It is the love of reverie—among
The unfrequented woods to brood alone
Till sweet thoughts rise like music, though the tongue
Keep mute for want of fitting speech and tone

To make their voiceless melody its own ;
Then in such mood the chastenings of the past—
Affections chilled, wrongs suffered, hopes o'erthrown,
Humbly review—till the deep shadow cast
Over the heart is gone, and peace dwells there at last.

XXXI.

Such is this love, and if it best inspire
The soul with sense of its own majesty,
The mind with noble aspiration fire,
And from the passions' slavery set it free ;—
Persuade the sceptic from his doubts to flee,
And (owning equally the chastening rod
And favouring smile of Nature's Deity)
Humbly to bow where scornfully he trod,—
Shall we not truly say—it is the love of God ?

XXXII.

If with no other, with this love at least
I go to join the world where I must strive,
And when this calm pause in it shall have ceased,
This sweet Oasis that has kept alive
A faith too feeble—may its thoughts survive
To keep my heart, amid life's desert, green,
And pure, and strong,—that if I fail or thrive—
Find sun or shadow in this mortal scene,
God may be felt through all, whate'er else intervene.

At Naples—1853.

I.

AGAIN I stand in Naples, and a scene
Of wondrous loveliness again look o'er ;
In *that* no change was needed, nor hath been,
But oh ! that freedom smiled upon its shore,
And that the despot darkened it no more
Whom flattering priests and flattered mobs obey !
Slaves—wretched slaves—such king who bow before,
Will none arise to check his blood-stained sway,
None raise a hand to sweep this Bourbon blight away ?

II.

Oh, who would fix his home in such a land,
Or from its charms could pleasure long derive ?
Farewell to sunny skies and breezes bland
Where Liberty can find no space to thrive,
Give me the soil where mind with mind may strive,
Free as its winds, though these may fiercely blow ;
Where spies and traitors find no golden hive,
Where justice waits alike on high and low,
And love with loyalty is ever seen to grow.

III.

But one such country do we yet behold,
No need to name *thee*, England ; world-confess'd
Is thy pre-eminence, and world-extolled ;
Nor to thy children only art thou blest,
No nation is there but doth manifest
Due rev'rence towards thee ; tyrants quail before
Thy knowledge of their deeds ; to thee the opprest
Of all lands fly—once harboured on thy shore,
No crowned oppressor dare pursue his victim more.

IV.

Naples, life's primest years have passed from me
Since first thy charms inspired my early verse,
With wiser mind do I revisit thee—
One which has learnt that trial is no curse,
That there is danger in the grief we nurse,
That work is health and duty too, that song
For nobler ends was given than to asperse
Man or his Maker ; that peace can ne'er belong
Unto the head or heart until the will be strong.

V.

This have I learned amid much care and sorrow,
Whose shadow ofttimes did my heart o'ercast,
Yet onward strove I, hopeful of the morrow,
Until the days of sunshine came at last,

7

And my hard struggle with the world was past.
Oh ! vision bright—to see life's sky all clear,
To hear no more adversity's keen blast
Sweep round my home—to love without a fear ;
And in the loved one's smile detect no lurking tear.

VI.

O vision brief ! though radiant to the close ;
Scarce bloomed the Paradise its light had made
Ere that dear smile departed—with the rose
Still on the cheek where its sweet sunshine played ;
Was I then left where *she* no longer stayed ?
What on my head such awful woe had brought ?
Stunned and o'erwhelmed I sank beneath its shade,
As if for me that " huge eclipse " were wrought
Which palsies at a blow, sense, action, feeling, thought !

VII.

I stood aghast—endeavouring to persuade
My wildered spirit that 'twas all a dream,
That—in some way—to her departed shade
Would come again life's vitalizing stream ;
And, for a time, her haunting form did seem
But as a statue that to life might wake
Like feigned Hermione's—through force supreme
Of deathless love its spectral silence break,
And to my longing arms give all they yearned to take.

VIII.

But ah ! for me what form was to descend
From pedestal that bore no counterfeit ?
Vainly did I my longing arms extend,
The statue stirred not ; no warm bosom beat
Like that which rose,—no unsubstantial cheat,—
To bless the lorn Leontes ; well I knew
I wooed but phantom of my own deceit,
Yet scarce deceit—'twas still reflection true
Of what was in my heart, though nothing met my view.

IX.

Slowly came glimpses of returning light,
Till to their 'customed aspect all things grew
With cruel sameness ; *they* had felt no blight,
Nor of the one upon my spirit knew ;
Clear lay the pathway I must still pursue,
Why did I pause ? stern duty cried, On ! on !
Alas, I knew life's work was still to do,
But how forbear the sad comparison
Of toil when *she* was here, and toil when she was gone ?

X.

Time and the chastener's hand that, striking, soothed.
Raised up at length my drooping heart and head,
And the world's ways, by prosp'rous fortune smoothed,
Offered kind welcome to my onward tread.

7– 2

More sufferings came, but there were none to dread,
This one survived—so passed by many a year—
Not by afflictive hours unvisited,
Yet bringing days whose sunshine still is here,
And may, perchance, endure life's later days to cheer.

XI.

Life's later days—I go back to a land
That gave me what I found not in my own,
My toil rewarding with a liberal hand ;
(Else had I not this healthful leisure known ;)
Yet when the days that end my toil have flown,
It is my hope to pass what few remain,
Within my native clime ; 'twill well atone
For my long exile thence, if spared the pain
Of parting from it more, when once my home again !

XII.

To Naples with this hope I bid farewell,
Nor care if now upon its sunny skies
I look my last ; content am I to dwell
'Neath those where mists, instead of mountains, rise
To shade the free land that beneath them lies ;
A land which still might more enlightened be,
Yet which its people's many needs supplies
As doth no other—let my choice be free,
And *that*, God willing, shall my final home here be.

England—1860.

I.

Iᴛ is accomplished; the mind-wearing toil
Which duty claimed, is ended; and again
My habitation is on English soil.
In Europe war still hovers, and the stain
Of other blood than battle's is too plain
In peaceful lands—too much upon my own;
Yet many evil things are on the wane;
Tyranny trembles, and the haughty tone
Of despots is so changed it scarcely seems their own.

II.

St. Elmo's cells are empty; Bomba sleeps
In one as dark; a despot—vile as he,
Heir to his throne, that throne no longer keeps:
Death and rebellion have combined to free
Naples from the detested tyranny
Of both; a patriot-hero has struck down,
To bloom no more, the Bourbon fleur-de-lis;
The Hapsburg dukes no longer wear a crown;
Venice alone remains in dread of Austria's frown.

III.

O Italy ! how little 'twas my thought,
When last I visited thy lovely land,
And marked the havoc which misrule had wrought,
That thy deliv'rance was so near at hand ;
May thy new-founded kingdom firmly stand,
And, once cemented 'neath Sardinia's sway,
Liberty's light throughout each part expand,
Till every shadow that upon thee lay,
By king or priest-craft cast, be scared, or sunned away !

Under the Cypress.

1841-46.

———◆◇◆———

GONE.

" And thou art dead, as young and fair,
　　As aught of mortal birth ;
And form so soft, and charms so rare
　　Too soon returned to earth ?

＊　　　＊　　　＊　　　＊　　　＊

I will not ask where thou liest low,
　　Nor gaze upon the spot,
There flowers or weeds at will may grow
　　So I behold them not—
To me there needs no stone to tell
'Tis nothing that I loved so well."—Byron.

I.

And *thou* art gone, not less deplored
　　Nor less beloved than she
Who woke Childe Harold's tenderest chord ;
　　Yet mourn I not as he,
I loved thee with too high a trust,
And love thee still—thou art *not* dust,
　　And dust shalt never be—
Whatever sceptic lips may tell,
'Tis *something* that I loved so well.

II.

And what was that I loved so well ?
   Was it the beauteous form
Now resting in its narrow cell,
   The breast no longer warm,
The voice that had so sweet a tone,
The eye that once so fondly shone—
   Did these contain the charm
That made me weep thy parting breath,
And binds me to thee still in death ?

III.

No !—these were but the clothing fair
   Of spirit robed for earth,
And destined all to perish *there*
   As things of mortal birth ;
Things that to me were very dear,
Tho' soon—too soon—to disappear ;
   Yet honoured for their worth
No more, when they no longer spoke
The inner light which through them broke.

IV.

It may be that, at first, there fell
   Despair's unthinking tear,
In gazing on the coffined shell
   Of pearl so bright and dear.

But Faith o'er sorrow's cloud soon threw
A light that shone with rainbow hue,
   Whilst Hope came smiling near,
And bade me look where angels dwell
For her that here I'd loved so well.

TOGETHER.

ONE evening 'twas, we sat alone,
Her gentle arms around me thrown,
(We, who had been for many a year,
In worldly phrase, a " married pair ").
I had come back to that dear home
From which I did but rarely roam,
After an absence which, though brief,
Had brought with it some shade of grief.
O'erjoyed she sat at my return,
Nor asked nor wished of else to learn.
Silent, I leant upon her breast,
Tasting at once love, joy, peace, rest.
Ah, they may smile at transports felt
By those who've at the altar knelt,
And many years are in advance
Of courtship's days of young romance ;
But when I think of that sweet eve,
And of my heart's contented heave,
I feel that wedded hearts and true
Taste bliss mere lovers never knew.

ALONE.

WHEN weary from the world I'd fly,
How sweet on thy dear breast to lie,
To feel thine arms around me folding,
And know 'twas thee mine own were holding!
Oh, thus, how oft I've sighed away
The cares and sorrows of the day,
And sunk, no word between us spoken,
Happy and mute, to rest unbroken.

Still weary from the world I fly,
But not on thy dear breast to lie,
No more thine arms are round me folding,
No longer thee mine own are holding.
A lonely pillow, sadly prest,
Is now my only place of rest,
Where, none to hear my grief if spoken,
I sink to sleep, no more unbroken.

NO LONGER HERE.

'Tis daybreak in the chamber where,
  A year ago, you died ;
And baby, as we call him still,
  Is sleeping by my side.
Morn after morn, I watch him wake,
  And not without a tear,
Can always bear to meet his smile
  Now thou'rt no longer here.

He nestles to me whilst my arms
  Around him fondly twine,
Until his cheek is resting where
  So oft hath rested thine ;
And, as my sighing heart-pants beat
  Beneath his little ear,
He little dreams the sigh's because
  Thou art no longer here.

He knows not yet, but soon will know,
  What means that mournful word
Which, coupled with his mother's name,
  He once unheeding heard.
God grant that when the knowledge comes
  He shed no bitter tear,
But I alone remain to grieve
  That thou'rt no longer here.

HER PORTRAIT.

YES, she was beautiful,
Gentle and dutiful,
In her brief life with me
Shunning all strife with me ;
For 'neath her cheerfulness
Lay depths of tearfulness,
And words uttered slightingly
Fell on her blightingly.

Oft would she walk with me,
Oft would she talk with me,
Setting me pondering
Whilst with her wandering ;
Full of serenity—
Full of amenity—
With a fond deference
Mingling her preference.

In her society
Ne'er was satiety,
Sweet was a word with her—
All who conferred with her,
Charmed by her suavity,
Touched by her gravity—
Came to her courtfully,
Went from her thoughtfully.

God-given wife to me,
Light of this life to me,
No more by side of me
(Pleasure and pride of me)
Fondly beholding thee—
Fondly enfolding thee—
Gentle, and dutiful,
Art thou, my beautiful!

One morn she woke not,
Spoke to, she spoke not—
Still she slept—seemingly—
Ah, 'twas *un*dreamingly;
Vainly we stayed by her,
Vainly we prayed by her,
Nought could awaken her—
Angels had taken her!

DAY AND NIGHT.

To lose the loved, if that were all,
   Brief suffering would cost;
But who shall free us from the thrall
   That makes us love the lost?

Who can his heart so coldly train
  Affection's links to wear,
Yet feel no pressure from the chain
  When gone, that once was there?

Why seem the flowers to sink to sleep
  So pensively at night,
The Sun's love in their hearts is deep,
  Tho' shut out from his light.
What are the moon and stars to them?
  His rays alone can dry
The tears that fall from leaf and stem
  That droop as tho' they'd die.

But they'll not die, those drooping flowers,
  Nor long their grief retain;
They do not dream of sunny hours
  That ne'er shall come again:
The Sun that left them for awhile,
  Shall soon again appear,
And make each weeping blossom smile
  The brighter for its tear.

But when the heart has lost its light
  From the beloved one's eyes,
Not sunset comes, but one long night
  Where morn no more shall rise.
Vain is the light of other hours,
  Unfelt their brightest ray,
Alas! the heart is like the flowers,
  It droops for want of *day!*

IN MEMORIAM SOROARIS.

I.

THOU, too, art gone ! oh, death's a wind
    That sweeps the gentlest flowers away,
Leaving the rude and rank behind
    As if they were too mean a prey ;
Ah, no ; all wither 'neath its blast,
But oft—too oft—the vilest last.

II.

Ah me ! how many a gap appears
    Along affection's golden chain ;
Well may I feel foreboding fears
    For the few links that still remain,
And tremble as they touch my heart
Lest they should, like the rest, dispart.

III.

Yet of such widely-severed links,
    Lamenting that they've grown so few,
Why is it that the heart still shrinks
    From filling up the chain with new ;
Nay—feels, at moments, loth to bear
The weight already hanging there ?

IV.

It is that death has taught the *cost;*
  With equal pride and joy are worn
The treasures that have ne'er been lost ;
  And readily that weight is borne
Which only presses on the heart
A thrill of rapture to impart.

V.

But when the links of love's full chain
  Have once been broken—oh, the breaking
Costs all too much to risk again
  An advent of such sad heart-aching ;
Of too much have we been bereft
To dare to add to what is left.

Sonnets.

PREFATORY.

In years mature, when those calm heights are won
    Which youth at such disheartening distance saw,
When the world's smiles we neither seek nor shun,
    And of its frown no longer stand in awe:
When we have learnt amid our fellow men,
    Of human sympathies the better part,
Striving the while from fruit of wisdom's pen
    To nobly feed the intellect and heart,—
May such a one, without presumption, think
    Some light is worth reflecting from his mind,
Or from his thought's free utterance shall he shrink
    Because his words may not warm welcome find?
Small heed, I know, this age accords to verse,
Yet let mine go—the world has borne with worse.

EVENING.

How beautiful this eve is !—Heaven and Earth
　Seem wrapped in fond communion.　All is still,
As if had come the first hours of the birth
　Of that new time, when peace the world shall fill !
O Nature, how sublime is thy repose !
　Not inapt emblem of the lofty soul
Which, in composure oft its best strength shows—
　The brave serenity of self-control,
The calm, not of prostration, but command ;
　The pause of power, not love or need of ease ;
Divine quiescence—such as the fine hand
　Of him, who wrought the resting Hercules,
Reveals in that majestic attitude
Of man's most noble form in man's most Godlike mood

———◆———

WORLD-FEAR.

The human heart how full of love and deep !
　Yet of its depths how little do we know ;
Near its earth-bordered margin still we creep,
　Ever afraid with its full tide to flow.
Like bathers, stand we on a river's brink,
Growing more cold the longer that we shrink ;
Or lie, like ships within a hostile port,
　Longing to slip our cables, and be free ;
But dare not for the world's o'erhanging fort
　That threatens all who would put out to sea.

Vain fear! The Framer of the human heart
    Gave it for good, an expanse deep and wide ;
In shallow feelings great souls take no part,
    Only small barks near shore securely ride !

PROGRESS.

PROGRESS!—The word is somewhat proudly spoken
    In these unhinging days of stir and strife,
When, if some idols lie for ever broken,
    Others, methinks, are gaining fresher life.
More love of luxury, more greed of gain,
    Old faiths renounced for any strange or new,
Or still professed, with logic on the strain
    To give the false the colour of the true.
Folly, and scarcely decency—in dress,
    Prize-fighters honoured, spirit-rappers owned,
Bacchus upheld in Pulpit—and in Press,
    For Jockeys' sport, the Senate's work postponed ;—
These may be signs of progress, but the end
Is yet to show us *whither* it will tend.

DOMENICHINO'S SIBYL.

Is this a poet's dream, the painter's art,
    Or prophet's spirit ?—or the concentration
Of all that beams from man's immortal part
    Embodied by his mortal, to creation ?

8—2

Beautiful shadow of the world ideal
   Communing silently with destiny,
The Sibyl's fore-knowledge was not unreal,
   If she who bore that name resembled thee.
The power of prescience is in thine eye,
   The might of intellect is on thy brow—
Thy brow of gentleness and majesty :
   Methinks before thee Wisdom's self might bow,
And her own soul, informed by thine, imbue
With deeper knowledge of the beautiful and true.

RISING TO FALL.

Some on life's course, like high-bred racers, start,
   Scorning the rein that would their neck be bending ;
Or, high in aim as that of bow-sped dart,
   Seem borne from earth, as if to heaven ascending.
Swift and impetuous, at first, they soar,
   Spite of all pressure 'gainst their strong intent ;
But, wavering soon, their skyward flight is o'er,
   And naught remains but sudden, sure descent.
Remember ye, who'd *keep* the height ye gain,
   Resolve, once pausing, like the arrow, falls—
That noblest impulse, without God, is vain,
   But who on Him, for help in weakness, calls,
May trust his pinions, wheresoe'er he flies,
Nor fear to sink however high he rise.

CONFORMITY.

"The world is too much with us."—WORDSWORTH.

'TIS but a lie to say He is our God
 Who falls and rises with the world's esteem.
Have we no fear of His avenging rod
 In such vile homage to the sole Supreme ?
How dare we stamp *His* name on each base coin
 Issued from Pilate's forge or Cæsar's mint,
Perceive the cheat, and yet the chorus join
 Which drowns their voices who the truth would hint ?
O hierarchy of custom ! 'neath thy sway
 Body and soul are clothed in strange misfits.
In shaping both we thy behests obey
 Till we have grown slaves, cowards, hypocrites,
And dare not, for this palsying dread of Thee,
Ourselves, in thought, or speech, or action, be.

TIME'S APOCALYPSE.

THERE is a seething movement mid mankind
 Which makes wise fools prophetic ; in the shock
Which the world feels, but portents dire they find,
 Or mysteries, whose secrets to unlock

They only are deputed ; sightless sages !
    Can they not see that all this stir and strife
Is but the growing fire of gathering ages ?
    The spirit bursting into fresher life
Of human progress—dowry of the past
    Unto the future, to shine brighter still
With each convulsion till succeeds the last ?
    The wider spreading feud of good with ill,
Of truth with falsehood—no such saddening sight,
For Might is wavering fast before the step of Right !

HEALTH.

O glorious health, a double life he lives
    Who lives with thee : he tramples down all care,
Takes fearlessly what liberal nature gives,
    And reaps in mind and body his full share.
What heedeth he if breezes sleep or blow ?
    His own pulse beats with a too buoyant swell
To care how those of wind or weather go ;
    The clouds for him no tale forbidding tell,
And the keen gust upon the breezy heath
    But brings him warmth of blood and strength of limb :
Sweet too, the contrast of soft summer's breath ;—
    In every season there is joy for him :
O thou who hast this blessing, hold it fast,
Few for us here remain when this is past.

SPECULATION.

Vain ponderings that bear away the mind
    Into the regions of entangling thought,
Till, like the fly in spider's web entwined,
    It feels its wings inextricably caught,
And, only struggling where it hoped to soar,
    Can neither find deliv'rance nor retreat.
Too curious mortal! why, oh, why explore
    Tracks where no knowledge can direct thy feet?
Keep on the course that wiser men have trod;
    Or if no traces of their steps appear,
Conscience, that surest finger-post of God,
    Shall point the way, and duty's path make clear;—
Conscience—the angel ever at our side
To be, when reason fails, our counsellor and guide.

INQUIRY.

Whence come we?—whither go we?—and the why
    And wherefore of this trial-scene of life
Are questionings which all, who wisely try,
    May wisely answer; not by mental strife,
    Nor probing creeds with which the world is rife,
But by acceptance of the light within
    Which, wordlessly, reflects the word divine;
And is to Revelation's self akin,

Shedding a brighter light on many a line
  Than doth from cloister, church, or college shine ;
God's word was destined wider spread to find
  Than Bible soil—He gave, of plainer page
An earlier scripture, meant for all mankind,
  And, without priestcraft, teaching every age.

CONVICTION.

RELIGION is a birth of the full heart
  Where, oft enwombed with restless throb, it lies
Until to life some angel bids it start,
  And ope, with baby gaze, its wondering eyes ;
  Then, guided in its new and sweet surprise
By Charity, Faith, Hope, it sees a world
From which, like curtain suddenly unfurled,
  Shadows, and clouds, and mists, dispersing, rise —
And strong in virtue's majesty and might—
  Of which the mind becomes the noble slave,
Goes forth accoutred for the Christian's fight,
  Becoming wise by being true and brave—
Finding out God, through hatred of all ill,
And perseverance in his heavenly will.

CREEDS.

WHAT is a creed? the despotism of mind
 O'er mind—the tyranny of intellect
That, save its own, all freeborn thought would bind;
 The bannered dogma 'neath which every sect
 Rejoicing in its militant career
Makes war on every other—in God's name,
But with such weapons as the fiend might claim.
 Discordant hierarchs—I've nor heart nor ear
For Faith, whose signs are mystery and strife,
 Whose problems reason strives in vain to solve—
No creed I hold, save from his lips and life
 Who gave it—not as preached in dull revolve
Of periodic twang that scarce can break
The slumber of the sense, still less the soul awake!

TO BACCHUS.

SEDUCTIVE demon! from my presence fly,
 For I abhor thee, tho' I own thy charm,
Take off from me that basiliscan eye
 Which, gazing thus, can only bode me harm.
Thou devil in fair shape! I know thee well,
 And all the ruin thou hast brought on earth
In hearts and homes which thou hast made a hell
 Under the guise of cheerfulness and mirth,

Giving smooth name to even murder's deed ;
   I know the texts with which thou canst deceive
Thy slaves into acceptance of thy creed,
   Till men who doubt all else, in thee believe.
Preachers who rave about the primal curse,
Tell me—is not this *latter one* far worse ?

DEATH.

FOND sufferer, come away ! nor feed thy gaze
   On looks which are not life's, nor ever were ;
Weep, if thou wilt, the ending of those days
   So near at hand when health, still glowing there,
Bespoke the present soul ; but linger not
   O'er the worn casket whence the jewel's gone,
Nor the sweet memories of life's moments blot
   By this sad *one* too darkly brooding on.
Its inmate fled—the house deserted lies ;
   No longer there, then, thy beloved one seek ;
The silent tongue, the inexpressive eyes,
   The pallid brow, the cold and hueless cheek—
Tell but the answered summons God has sent
To call the tenant from his mortal tenement.

BURIAL.

WHY all this care for decomposing dust—
    This pageantry in honour of the clay
That breathes no more ?   Why is it that we must
    This wretched tribute to vile custom pay,
    As each poor body in the earth we lay ?
Feathers, and silk, and velvet—how I hate
    The sight of the theatrical display,
To see the sashed stipendiaries that wait
    The signal for their faces to look grave,
And their mute tramp beside the hearse commence !
    Why for such mockery our ashes save ?
Surely the burning pile were less offence
    That left no single vestige of the dead,
    Than all this pomp to grace a case of oak and lead !

———◦◇◦———

THE GRAVE.

I WANDERED thro' the churchyard, pondering much
    Upon the falsehoods which the tombstones told,
Infidel falsehoods—for I deem them such
    That vitalize what charnel-houses hold.
" Here sleeps "—" here rests ! " appalling words, if true.
    For sleep is life, and life within the grave
Methinks were blessing coveted by few ;
    Ev'n for eternal slumber in the cave

Of Death, *repose* were a most lying word.

    Not in such rest abides the " Peace of God ; "
Not in such rest are angel voices heard.

    No ; the cold dust beneath the churchyard's sod
Has done with slumber ; neither mortals sleep,
Nor souls immortal rest, where worms their banquet keep.

THE TRUE PRINCE.

IN MEMORIAM ALBERTI.

I.

O union blest, when title, state, and wealth
    Fall to his lot who, unto noble heart,
Joins lofty mind ; who, ev'n in youth and health,
    Prince though he be, dares play the Christian's part ;
Doing no act, save what is good, by stealth.
    Student no less of each refining art,
Than of the knowledge that makes goodness wise ;
    Endeavouring in every worldly aim,
In God's esteem as well as man's to rise,
    And fearing Him before all earthly shame
Save shame itself; abhorring all disguise,
    To servile praise preferring honest blame.
Such Prince, though sprung from no illustrious line,
Who would deny were one by right divine ?

II.

Such wert thou, Albert !—and if history—true
    To her great ends—have other tales to tell
Than how Ambition doth base aims pursue,
    How nations warred, how statesmen rose and fell ;
If, beside telling us what blood was spilled
    On battle-fields, it be her pride to note
In peaceful times when stations high were filled
    Greatly and worthily ; would she devote
Her pen to record of more grateful themes
    Than task it in the wearisome detail
Of party feuds, or politician's schemes ;—
    Thine's a career on which she cannot fail
To linger fondly, pausing till she give
Place to it in her page where names immortal live !

III.

The shadow of thy loss is on us yet,
    And with its burden overbears our pride ;
Nor can we her far deeper woe forget,
    Who found in thee friend, husband, guardian, guide.
With and for her we weep ; but when the first
    Gush of our sorrow shall have passed away,
When time to calmer feeling shall have nurst
    Our instant grief ; ungrateful were delay

To make our glorying in thy virtues known ;
    To tell the world, with unreluctant lips,
What, while thou liv'dst, they did but tamely own.
    But good deeds never suffer long eclipse,
And thine, as now into full light they start,
Shall fit memorial have from Britain's hand and heart.

IN MEMORIAM FRATRIS.

HE died in prime of manhood, not without
    Repute beyond what he had hoped to gain,
Yet full of cares success could not shut out
    From a too anxious heart and chafing brain.
    The intellect, whose wit's too ready vein
Won folly's laugh, and wisdom's kindly smile,
Fretted for loftier office ; and the while
    The world applauded, he, with self-disdain,
Oft from his work recoiled ; for in him lay
    Capacity of nobler toil and thought
Than wake the utterance that suits the day,
    And 'twas his hope, ere dying, to have wrought
A monument of more enduring fame
Than that which links the " comic " with his name.

THE DINNER CONTROVERSY.

Something too much of this ! When paupers die
　　Year after year for want of *any* food,
How Dives eats, or what his cooks supply,
　　To hear—I am not in a patient mood.
The science which can bring a single meal
　　Cheaper or better to the half-fed poor,
Make them less keenly hunger's nippings feel,
　　Or keep gaunt famine longer from their door,
Shall have my ready ear ; but to be told
　　Of thirteen *plats*, " each with its kindred wine,"
Served " one by one," that " none be eaten cold ; " *
　　And at a cost for which the poor might dine
By scores—revolts me, and with shame I burn
　　That Christian men should care such *gourmandise* to
　　　　learn.

"L'EMPIRE C'EST LA PAIX."

" My empire's peace," thus the French Emperor spoke,
　　And half the world began to rave and rail
Because his promise he so quickly broke ;
　　No doubt 'tis shocking, Royalty should fail

* *Vide* letter to *The Times.*

To keep its word; but what good Christians *we*
　　To feel such anger at deceit of kings;
How pure the heart, how sound the faith must be
　　From whence such righteous indignation springs.
Grave hypocrites! do we no pledges break—
　　Not unto man but to his Maker made?
No unkept vows in church or chapel take
　　That thus our hate of falsehood we parade?
" My empire's peace: " why, so said God's dear Son,
And yet we go to war and cry, " Thy will be done."

THE HOUSELESS POOR—A CHRISTMAS APPEAL.

THE houseless poor! sad words, and sadder still
　　Their truthful utterance in a Christian land;
Think of it ye who cheerful homes yet fill,
　　Till your touched hearts arouse a helping hand!
The houseless poor! Ah, poverty alone
　　Is no light burden; but when shelterless
It roams the streets to give out there the moan
　　Of pain and anguish, only they can guess
Its pangs who bear them; wake, ye prosperous, wake
　　To recognition of the want and woe
That shiver round you, and for Christ's dear sake
　　Let them no more unsought, unsheltered go,
But gather them, ere comes the wintry night
Where they may refuge find, if but till morning's light.

SUGGESTED BY READING THE AMERICAN REJOICINGS ON THE LAYING DOWN OF THE ATLANTIC CABLE.

I.

WHY this o'erflowing joyaunce? are they dreams
　Or sober truths of which we have been told?
What is accomplished? any of His schemes
　Who gave the faith our shouting brethren hold?
What is the glorious work that has been done,
　Transporting half a world beyond itself—
A conquest on no field of battle won,
　A victory without the strife of pelf?
Why those divine words uttered: " Peace on earth,
　Good-will towards men " from voices jubilant,
As if Christ's empire, brought to sudden birth,
　Were ruling now with sway predominant;
What means it all—it means that o'er the sea
Two mighty nations blend their voices lovingly.

II.

'Tis well, two nations of one faith and tongue
　Conjoined by links that make them one in heart!
'Tis well for this a song of joy is sung;
　Yet brethren are there whom no oceans part
Standing aloof with unfraternal eye,
　On either shore, which these great nations boast;
Whom to unite by never-breaking tie,
Still higher feat were than from coast to coast

9

To stretch the wire electric ;—I would not
   A noble work disparage, or decry ;
Let fame. to whom the merit's due. allot
   Her fitting wreath ; but let us tell no lie—
Commerce and science wrought the work we view,
But Christianity's is *yet* to do.

———◆———

JONATHAN'S WELCOME TO OUR PRINCE.

AY, *these* are sounds from a great nation's heart
   In whose outpouring is no base alloy ;
No actor here exaggerates his part,
   This is no burst of mercenary joy,
But of a country's one accordant soul
   Giving its noblest, kindest feelings vent,
Displaying nought 'twere wiser to control.
   Impulsive people ! never reticent
Of aught that stirs thy spirit—good or ill—
   Long may this fervent concentrated shout
Of welcome to our Prince our bosoms thrill ;
   Nor let the memory of its ringing out
Cease to thrill thine—till bonds too strong to part—
Firmer than shore to shore—shall join us heart to heart.

———◆———

ON READING IN *THE TIMES* NEWSPAPER AN ACCOUNT OF THE PRIZE-FIGHT BETWEEN SAYERS AND HEENAN.

HENCE with the nauseous details, hence !—and shame
    To any press, whate'er its motive be,
Which to the world could laudingly proclaim
    This feat of gladiatorial butchery ;
Shame to the stalwart hirelings fed and trained,
    Like human game cocks, for the brutal sport ;
Shame to the purse which gave the gold they gained ;
    Shame to the pens which gave their strife report ;
Shame to the humblest roofs or noblest halls
    Where with applause the noxious tale was read ;
Shame to the tongue which " manly courage " calls
    Display of strength, debasing heart and head ;
And to the countries which have stooped to claim
Two bruisers for their champions—doubly, trebly—*shame.*

SUGGESTED BY THE CONVICTION AND EXE-CUTION OF JOHN BROWN.

I.

SUCCESS, thou art a god which well may boast
    Homage denied " Jehovah, Jove, or Lord ! "
For each of these commands a separate host ;
    But thee *all* worship with combined accord.

Poor Brown! brave wearer of a humble name,
    Hadst thou struck down the slaves thy hand set free,
Or with some bloody conquest linked thy fame,
    Small ill thy rulers would have spoke of thee.
Yet in thy fall thy *cause* is not o'erthrown—
    A cause in which 'twere nobler far to die,
E'en on the scaffold, than to mount a throne
    By trampling on a nation's liberty.
Ham's prisoner is France's Emperor now;
But, in the eye of Heaven, which stands greater, he or
    thou ?

II.

Trial, conviction, and the awful lull
    'Twixt doom and death have passed.   A mightier State
Had spared his life ; but to be merciful
    Slave-rulers dared not.   He hath met his fate.
He erred : but let his motive and his cause
    From ridicule or scorn his memory shield.
Nor class him with those rebels to our laws—
    The skulking braggarts of the cabbage-field—
Who, pestilent traitors as they were, were spared
    To rave forth more sedition ; and (the doom
Escaping which they merited) meanly dared
    To spit in face of pardon.   From *their* tomb
Freedom, recoiling, with contempt shall turn,
But ne'er unweeping pass, poor Brown, thy humbler urn.

GARIBALDI AT ASPROMONTE.

FOILED in his great, but vain and rash attempt,
   The hero's sword is stricken from his hand ;
He falls—not quite from rebel's guilt exempt
   But true and faithful to his native land,
Which hails him still her dearest, noblest child !
   Though, in her cause, by his impatient heart,
And others' schemes too readily beguiled
   To deeds of which she sometimes feels the smart.
Deal with the great man greatly—he has erred ;
   And captive, wounded, on a bed of pain
Awaits the penalty he has incurred ;
   Let it be light, and may he ne'er again
Peril the loss of all that he hath won
By striving to achieve what best were left undone.

NORTH AND SOUTH.

"A plague on both your houses."—*Romeo and Juliet.*

I.

THE gathering clouds of years, at length, have risen,
And burst in direful storm upon thy land,
O haughty race ! that, whip and chain in hand,
Hast made of God's free soil the negro's prison :—

Holding the creed, for pen and tongue to teach,
That liberty is not the due or good
Of Afric's sons ; whilst he in peril stood
Who dared the odious doctrine to impeach ;
Doctrine alike of platform, pulpit, Press
Shouting in chorus the stupendous lie—
That, by the fiat of the One most High,
The slave *is* slave—that Jesus left, no less
Than Moses, Scripture-warrant for their right
Who hold the black man bondman to the white !

II.

Proud State ! had hate of this revolting creed
Grown with the heat of thy continued strife—
We had less blushed to see thy country bleed ;
But till thy slaughters bring to life and light
More noble aims than yet have prompted those
In race, in country, and in faith allied,
To war with all the hate of deadliest foes—
Ask not our sympathy for either side !
Not for the South—quite ready still to burn
The slave who'd struggle from his chains to fly ;
Not for the North—that from that slave would turn,
E'en at Christ's altar, if he came too nigh.
We can but pray the feud of both will cease,
Severed for ever now—despite of War or Peace.

MINOR POEMS.

—◦◇◦—

Freedom.

"How often have we heard 'The rights of man? Hurra!
The sovereignty of the people! Hurra!' roared out by men
who, if called upon in another place, and before another audience,
to explain themselves, would give to the words a meaning, in
which the most monarchical of their political opponents would
admit them to be true, but which would contain nothing new,
or strange, or stimulant, nothing to flatter the pride or kindle
the passions of the populace."—COLERIDGE.

Ay, Freedom is a high and glorious aim,
Yet for itself our reverence may not claim ;
But as a means by which we learn to bind
The body to the service of the mind ;
Thought, action, language, that we these may use
As gifts from God—too rich to tamely lose ;
For ends like these, it frets me not to hear
The people told that " Liberty is dear."

But that for which a rampant rabble cry,
And, if you asked them, could not tell you, *why,*

Caught by those claptraps for huzzaing praise
Which ev'ry brawler from the hustings brays,
Bleating them forth as if he'd just found out
Some great " Eureka " hitherto in doubt,
And laboured, like the bellman, by his throat,
To set the grand discovery afloat—
Those raving shouts, enough one's ear to crack,
Bellowed by knaves for fools to echo back,
Have nought to do with Liberty—that word
Means something else when *only* that is heard.

" Ah, Freedom ! " well did Roland's wife exclaim,
" What crimes has man committed in thy name ! "
Yet, with a touch of not unworldly pride,
For liberty that noble lady died :
Ev'n she, amid that moral whirlwind tost,
In which the bravest and the best were lost,
Deemed freedom virtue—and the cheat survives
To shed a halo round less worthy lives.
Oh, the great truth has yet to be received,
That *virtue's freedom*—'tis but half believed,
Save by the few of high, yet humble mind,
Who, in that truth, no earth-fame care to find.

Yes, virtue's freedom—teach the poor man this,
Ye demagogues, and ye'll not prate amiss ;
Tell him, though kings and taxes were no more,
A mightier tyrant still would press him sore ;
Tell him too—though it tickle not all ears,
'Tis the sole tyrant that the brave man fears,

And the sole tyrant God hath bid him kill.
Against this despot arm him, if you will,
And let at once Rebellion's work begin
Against the ruthless tyranny of sin:
O'er this triumphant, though *they* still remain—
Taxes and kings will give him little pain,
And he will learn that there are things more dear
Than vote by ballot, or his pot of beer.

Yes, virtue's freedom—freedom and content
Beyond all harm from State-mismanagement;
Thus clothed, the poor man may hold on his way,
Nor heed what club or hustings babblers say,
Secure, in self-respect, and self-control
From ev'ry fetter that can reach the soul;
Whoe'er shall strive this freedom to extend,
Will be indeed the poor man's truest friend,
Nor less his country's—though the patriot's name,
He ne'er may win; yet which may that best claim—
He who hath gained new kingdoms for the State,
Or he who helps to make its people good and great?

Evil Genius.

WHAT is the bard's most high vocation ?
    To rankle the wounds of grief and wrong,
Till suffering grow to exasperation
    Beneath the breath of his burning song ?
To stir up the blood of the poor man's heart,
    Till he looks upon wealth as his direst foe,
And deems that he acts but the hero's part
    In laying each hated Dives low ?

Or divinelier sounds the poet's verse
    To the tune of his own dark discontent—
Smothered in tones 'twixt a sneer and a curse,
    For this was the heaven-born minstrel sent ?
Never like this sang bard divine,
    And the harp that can only give forth such strains,
Is pernicious and false as the critic's line
    That aids in the ill-won praise it gains.

In Vino Falsitas.

GRIEF banished by wine will come again,
  And come with a deeper shade,
Leaving, perchance, on the soul a stain
  Which sorrow had never made :
Then fill not the tempting glass for me,
  If mournful, I will not be mad ;
Better sad, because we are sinful, be,
  Than sinful because we are sad.

Cease then to act the tempter's part,
  Nor ask me to drink again
Of that which can only cheer my heart
  By stealing away my brain ;
Pleasant is warmth when the wintry air
  Makes us shiver—but who'd not avoid
The blazing hearth—if what drew him there
  The limbs, which it warmed, destroyed ?

Burns' Centenary (1858).

Why all this noise because the hundredth year
Is come since Burns first saw this mortal sphere?
What added glory can attend his name
In being dragged down from the heights of fame,
To be passed round at dinner-tables, spread
For boozing guests at one pound one per head?
Might not the demonstration, too, be spared,
When we reflect how Burns, when living, fared?
That e'en this moment, at the crowded font
Of Charity, his daughter waits in want,
Hoping that those may give the living bread
Who banquets join in honour of the dead.*

But if the world, reminded by a date,
Departed genius must commemorate,
Is that of Burns the only radiant name
Which glitters in the calendar of fame?
Shines *Milton's* there so dubious or so dim
That no centenary is due to him—
Who taught his country, both in song and speech,
In loftier strains than Scotia's bard could reach,
And who, to virtue as to genius, true,
Showed in himself the greatness that he drew?

---

* There was an advertisement in *The Times*, side by side with
that relating to the Centenary, soliciting help for the destitute
and only daughter of the poet.

But were Burns' life (whose is ?) without defect,
Sure he himself this homage would reject,
He would have felt that genius, truly bright,
Wanted no showman to display its light,
That Fame deserved would still be Fame without
Perpetual or periodic shout,
And (for none shrunk with more disgust than he
From o'erwrought praise or fulsome flattery),
Would have disdained, to feed his country's pride,
Tribute or rank to higher worth denied.

The Law of Nations.

"My noble friend says that General Garibaldi has assumed
his position in violation of the law of nations. All I can say
is, that if the law of nations is to be enforced to effect perpetual
subjugation and misery in any nation, the sooner we hear as
little as possible of the law of nations the better."—*Extract from
Lord Brougham's Speech.*

WELL said, brave Brougham! thy speech has oft con-
    founded Freedom's foes,
But never in more timely words or thrilling strains than
    those;
Let every despot be, who pleads the law of nations, told,
Such law in aid of Might o'er Right will England never
    hold.

Away with all this reticence that timid statesmen ask,
This veiling of a nation's scorn 'neath diplomatic mask ;
Let's say at once we'll make no bows to wearers of a
    crown,
Who claim, by royal right, to strike or hunt their subjects
    down.

Outspoken, like our brave old Brougham, let every Briton
    be—
Wherever tyrants rise or fall—against their tyranny ;
Nor covertly be breath'd one prayer for triumph of the
    cause
Which from the scabbard parts the sword a Garibaldi
    draws.

Adventurer they call him, eh ?   Well, let the stigma be,
Let's have some more adventurers, if all be such as he ;
Humanity will welcome them wherever they bear sway,
Nor nations, haply, fare the worse whose kings they
    sweep away.

The Warsaw Conference.

WHAT are the despots doing
    Who have at Warsaw met,
What plans are they pursuing,
    Whose schemes would they abet ?

Who sought this new communion
   These monarchs three would frame,
What blessing from *their* union
   Can come or ever came?

Has Sicily's uprising
   Against its tyrant lord,
Set their sage heads devising
   How he may be restored?
Or do their proud hearts tremble,
   King, Emperor, and Czar,
Lest their fate his resemble
   Who *was* what yet they are?

Is Italy's alliance
   Beneath Sardinia's wing
A challenge of defiance
   To every Northern king?
Then why these consultations?
   To find some plea for Might
To turn the law of Nations
   Against the law of Right?

Oh, Germany! shortsighted
   To Freedom's spreading ray,
Oh, Russia! too long plighted
   To Autocratic sway;
League, if ye will, together;
   The liberty you'd blight
Has seen its stormiest weather,
   And shines each day more bright.

On Reading "The Song of the Pen" in the Dublin University Magazine.

MINSTREL, who singest of the Pen,
Sing to us the like again !
Tell us more of those visions bright,
That shine on the bard in the lonely night ;
Colouring his thoughts with that heavenly hue
Which reflecteth the beautiful and true—
For beautiful and true indeed
Hold I to be the poet's creed !

Yet, let that Pen do what it can
To tell the glorious creed to man ;
By few will its oracles be received,
Well understood, or well believed,—
For it is like all divinest things,
Too pure for men's imaginings ;
And some will scoff, and some will sneer
Whenever its high-priests appear.
    And they who follow the better choice,
    Of listening to the " charmer's voice "—
    Forget, when to the world returned,
    The holy lessons they have learned.

Yet, some there are, who not in vain
   Drink in the poet's full outpourings ;
Nor trace to a distempered brain,
   His wildest themes, or highest soarings.
And I am one who from the first
   Hour of my spirit's upward turning—
Its lessons in my heart have nurst,
   And loved beyond all other learning.
And one too am I, who have known the pain
Of the struggle betwixt the pen and the brain—
And the brain and the world—but 'twill e'er be so
Whilst the ink of the mind for bread must flow—
Emptying, perchance, its richest vein
For what well thou callest " a beggarly gain. "

   Yet, let none droop who wield the pen,
   But with those " many gifted men "
       Who have sung and said
       For their daily bread—
   What angels gladly would have read ;
   Hold on their course, and like the bird,
   Whose note in storm and cloud is heard—
   Rise upward still, and show how song
   Can triumph over want and wrong !

10

Francesca da Rimini.

Francesca! the immortal Florentine,
Who sings thy fall in his most moving line,
Hath linked thy name with love and poesy
Rather than shame and sorrow—made by thee,
Mourning is music—and, tho' we accost
Thy spirit mid the regions of the lost,
Pity and sympathy o'er all prevail
In listening to thy sad and simple tale ;
Oh, touchingly and beautifully sung ;
What ear could list uncharmed—what heart unwrung ?

I have looked on that same fair river's water,
Which, at the feet of Guido's gentle daughter,
Flowed as she sat by Paulo's arm embraced,
Upon that fatal day, when love had chased
From either breast all thought of else beside,
Till both were lost in passion's whelming tide.
And, musing there upon their mournful tale,
Have seemed to hear their spirit's moaning wail
Reproaching the soft lay and sunny clime
That taught their hearts, thro' love, to let in crime—
Too sunny clime—well might thy warmth betray
And through the senses steal the soul away—
Too thrilling lay—to hearts already flame
Thy tones, like incense, all too kindling came.

Sweet Italy !—yet let me blame thee not !
In colder climes will passion spread its blot,
And for thy language, if, at times there be
In its soft sounds too much of witchery—
Hearts like Francesca's had been safe from wrong,
Albeit in Dante's clime—inspired by Dante's song.

The Return of Spring.

IMITATED FROM GUARINI'S " PASTOR FIDO."

In freshest youth thou comest back, sweet Spring,
  As 'twere thy primal birth,
And, for the first time, thou wert scattering
  Thy glory over earth.
Yes, back *thou* comest—garden, field, and grove
  Thy joyous aspect wear,
And gay birds fill, where happy lovers rove,
  With melody, the air.
Yes, thou returnest, but with thee, O Spring !
  To me no more returns
The one dear smile beyond thy power to bring—
  Oh, for that smile how yearns
This aching heart ! fain would I welcome thee,
But ah ! love's light is fled—and what is *thine* to me ?

The Alpine Torrent.

FROM on high, from on high you see it pouring,
Windingly, shiningly, down it bends;
From afar, from afar, you hear it roaring,
Louder the noise as the stream descends;
Now through worn crevices silently creeping,
Now o'er a precipice haughtily leaping,
It goes with an endless chain.
Where is it gone?
The sound keeps on,
With a murmuring refrain;
'Tis but a moment lost in the pines,
But onward and earth-ward it still inclines—
Now we behold it again,
Swifter and fiercer its flow,
In the ray of the sunbeam brightly flashing,
Whirling—moaning—plunging—crashing
Down through the rent cliff's wildly dashing
Into the depths below:
The rocks may stem—the avalanche fall,
It bounds over avalanche, rocks and all,
Away—away—for ever away—
Like a bloodhound after its flying prey,
Down—still down—till on some low shore
Its sound is lost, and 'tis seen no more.

Does it not tell, that torrent's roll,
The tale of many a sunken soul ?
Of spirits which, though on virtue's height,
Kept still too much the world in sight,
Till down among the rocks they fell
Up which they'd climbed their way so well—
And taking then a downward course,
Could stem no more sin's torrent-force,
But wildly let it bear them on
Till Hope, and with it Fear, had gone !

England's Chivalry.

I.

Who says the heroic age is past, or that we must go back
Unto the olden time the steps of chivalry to track ?
All honour to the valour which our steel-clad knights displayed
Who lived among the stirring days of Tourney and Crusade ;
But search the record of those days, and search we shall in vain,
For deeds like those on Lucknow's walls, or Balaclava's plain.

II.

No, chivalry is with us still, by fiercer foes confessed
Than ever put in ages past its mettle to the test ;
Less picturesque its arms may be than battle-axe or lance,
Less meet, perchance, its heroes' names for epic or
          romance ;
Yet Havelock's is only one mid England's warrior throng,
Whose names would shed a glory o'er the bard's divinest
          song.

III.

Oh, every Christian gentleman will love the peaceful part,
But, knight or churl, in Britain's sons still beats the lion
          heart,
And roused at duty's call we've seen 'twill nerve his hand
          to do
More brilliant deeds than Agincourt or Cressy ever knew ;
Yes, chivalry still treads our land, with daring as sublime
And spirit nobler, purer far, than in the olden time.

Now and Then.

Do you remember when we walked
     One eve along this shore,
And of those hopes and feelings talked
     That move us now no more ?

The wind had sunk—the murmuring wave
　　Fell solemn, deep, and low,
Till, like the music which it gave,
　　Our converse seemed to flow.

With bygone years is that sweet eve,
　　And either heart since then
Of many a hope hath taken leave
　　That ne'er will rise again.
But if some lights no longer stay
　　That once illumed our track,
Some shadows too have passed away
　　That will no more come back.

Yes, gentle friend, no more we sail
　　A breeze-uplifted sea—
Rejoicing in the rising gale,
　　And bounding buoyantly.
But safer we've our bark in hand,
　　And, tho' life's winds decline,
Are nearing fast the better land
　　Beneath a breath divine.

To a Young Friend.

LILLY, thou wert but a child
When upon thee first I smiled,
Yet there is about thy face
Much that then I loved to trace :
'Tis more thoughtful, 'tis more fair,
Tells perchance of bygone care ;
But the softness infantine
Which thou then hadst—still is thine ;
Still dost thou, in voice and feature,
Seem the same sweet artless creature !

But, though thou art thus to me,
All will not so look on thee ;
Many in thy form and face
Will the budding woman trace,
And be seeking to inspire
Thy young breast with love's soft fire
Long before 'twere well to roam
From thy widowed mother's home ;
Or thy mind could act its part
In the guidance of thy heart.

Lilly ! let no suitor get
Of that heart possession yet,
Not for ever needst thou be
In " maiden musing fancy free,"

Thou wilt have enough unrest
When Love grows a timely guest,
But, in these thine earlier years,
Better hopes and wiser fears,
Trust me, may engage thy heart
Than any born of Cupid's dart.

Resignation.

I HEAR them tell of broken hearts
  And cheeks turned pale by sorrow's shade,
As if, when Hope's bright tint departs,
  Health's colours too were sure to fade ;
Ah, no—when all is dark below
The eye will smile, the cheek will glow.

Yet let none say, the loved and lost
  Are mourned the less by those who give
No sign of what dark shades have crost
  Their hearts, but on in patience live,
And trust, altho' life's sun hath set,
Some rays may gild its pathway yet.

Oh, no, tho' lost life's dearest charm,
  Life's duties still remain to do,
For these the heart should still keep warm,
  The mind still to its course keep true ;
And tho' the heart be darkened ground,
Peace soon shall shed its light around.

Parting.

E'en as ships diverge at sea
   Which together left the land,
Though to one port bound they be,
   And are by the same winds fanned—
Thou and I must now divide
   Whom was nothing once between—
Fare-thee-well, for side by side
   We shall never more be seen.

Earth is not our final port,
   Farther still our haven lies—
Where the tempest does not sport
   Nor the clouds bedim the skies.
On that far eternal shore
   Our fond souls shall mingle yet,
There we'll meet to part no more—
   Here, 'twas but to part, we met.

The Peasant's Home.

THE sky is bright, the scenes are fair
    Thro' which I haste along,
The sheep send out a joyful bleat,
    The birds a merry song ;
And other steps might linger here,
    But mine would onward roam,
For down in yonder valley lies
    My own beloved home.

For daily wants that must be met
    That home I daily leave,
And unto labour give the hours
    That pass 'twixt morn and eve—
O happiness, when they are fled—
    And I again am free
To gaze on those beloved ones
    Who long to gaze on me.

I feel as I'd a journey been
    Though each day I return,
And for the lips I kissed at morn
    At eve as fondly yearn ;—
O sacred blessings of the hearth,
    That wife and children share ;
Wherever else my brow is sad,
    I'm always happy *there*.

The Blind Man's Dying Farewell.

I KNOW thy tears are starting
  Although I see them not,
You weep that we are parting,
  Yet why bewail my lot ?
I go where fairer visions
  Will to my sight appear
Than have been hidden from me
  Throughout my darkness here.

Earth was not all a prison,
  Thy kindness made it bright,
But on my spirit risen
  Will beam celestial light.
And I from heaven will view thee
  With love become divine,
And be there thy good angel
  As thou hast here been mine.

Dejection.

WEARY'S my body, weary too my brain,
  Weary my heart, oh, fold me, gentle sleep,
Within thine arms, and let me there remain
  In slumber long and deep!

There have been hours when, as I lay awake,
  I dreamed of Heaven till Earth seemed far away.
But on me now such vision will not break
  The clog I feel of clay.

Pain, sleeplessness, I oft have borne before,
  And murmured not.   I do not murmur now,
But only sigh because I bear no more
  Unruffled heart and brow.

Pity my weakness, Thou who seest me lie
  With this unquiet mind,
Calm it to rest, or let me close mine eye,
  And peace in slumber find.

Retrospect.

A SIMPLE phrase is " long ago,"
　　But oh! how much it means,
Alike to manhood and to age,
　　And youth yet in its teens.
None, none are found so full of joy
　　That memory hath not power
To cast her shadow o'er the light
　　That gilds the present hour!

And soon the shadow falls.　　Not far
　　In life we wander on
Before we find some charm is missed,
　　Some hope at starting, gone!
And many a turning soon is passed
　　In which we fain would stay,
If time and duty did not call
　　Our steps another way.

And sadder still—perchance our road
　　Has here and there been blessed
With dear companions, and with *one*
　　More dear than all the rest!
But, long before our journey's o'er,
　　Those dear ones all have gone;
And left us, many a weary mile,
　　Alone to travel on!

Yet, 'tis not well to ponder thus
    On what no more can be,
Or wish that otherwise had been
    Our earthly destiny.
The pilgrim, who the future views
    With faith's unswerving eye,
Both past and present sorrow holds
    Worth no abiding sigh.

Calm and content he forward moves,
    To any fate resigned,
Not without shadows at his heart,
    But none upon his mind.
There shines a beam he prizes more
    Than love's or friendship's light,
A source, he knows, will never fail
    Of sunshine pure and bright.

Tempest.

One summer night I lay awake
    When storm was in the air,
Darkening my sight to make less bright
    The lightning's vivid glare.

But thro' my pressing hands I still
    Beheld its piercing flash, ˙
And, spite my muffled ear, still heard
    The thunder's awful crash.

Thus from truth's flash we strive to flee,
    And conscience' voice to drown,
But cannot from the one escape,
    Nor hush the other down.
The spiritual storm keeps on,
    Not, haply, to depart
Till it has left a clearer mind,
    And a less clouded heart.

Hope—Bear—Trust.

Hope! there is healing in sorrow's cup,
    Thousands of flowers now drop on their stem
Too tearful, too sunk to the sky to look up,
    But that sky with a smile still looks down upon them.

Bear! on life's ocean winds will fail,
    As they do to many a barque at sea,
But better such pause than the flying sail
    Where the helm has no longer the mastery.

Trust! the sigh of the Autumn breeze
  May be sad, and still sadder the wintry gust,
But the lonelier then grow the stricken trees,
  The nearer they are to Spring time—Trust!

—•◦•—

The Rivals.

A SWISS ANECDOTE.

From yonder mead, that gently slopes
  To Uri's smiling lake,
What merry sounds the silence of
  This sweet-breathed evening wake;
The village youth are gather'd there,
  For talk, and dance, and song,
All but the lovely Rosalie—
  Why joins not *she* the throng?

An old man in the churchyard sits
  Beside a maiden fair,
Displaying him a new-twined wreath
  With conscious beauty's air;
Yet, sad as lovely, seems her brow,
  Now there the wreath is placed,
And 'neath that calm, proud smile, a heart
  All restless may be traced.

11

" Hark, Rosalie ! " the old man cries,
    " Dost hear the merry lute,
Why linger here, apart from all,
    So mournful and so mute ?
Go, join the throng—in passing through,
    I heard some swains there say—
How fair our maids this eve, but ah !
    The *fairest* is away ! "

" Ha ! say'st thou so ? " the maiden cried,
    With eyes of sudden light,
" And what has dimmed then Isbel's charms
    That *mine* have grown so bright ?
Hath my brief absence from these scenes
    That matchless beauty shown,
She rules not o'er the hopes and hearts
    Of Uri's swains alone ? "

" Yes, Isbel now must yield the palm,"
    The old man sighed and said,
" No rival now, we all must own,
    Hath Rosalie to dread ;
Go smile—thy brighter eyes shall heal
    Each wound that Isbel's gave ;
Nor fear thy triumph will be brief,
    We sit on *Isbel's grave !* "

By the Sea-Side.

THE shade's on the turf
  Where it slopes to the ocean,
The wave without surf,
  And the wind without motion;
And the sun sinks to rest
  With a smile on the billow,
As I would on thy breast
  Might I make it my pillow.

Oh, tremble not so
  At the fond wish thou hearest,
Unfulfilled let it go,
  If to grant it thou fearest;
Nay, heed not the light,
  None are nigh to behold us,
And soon will the night
  In its shadow enfold us.

Timidity.

THE breeze that lifts thy drooping hair,
   And breathes upon thy cheek,
So softly sighing that it seems
   Some tender vow to speak,
Will wander, ere the sun has set,
   To other cheeks than *thine*,
Yet there its lips a welcome meet
   Ne'er granted yet to mine.

Shall I be bold, and, like the breeze,
   Whilst thus thy ringlets wave,
Bring my fond breath as near thy cheek
   And give the kiss it gave?
Alas! like leaves around their flower
   I tremble all too much,
And feel, like them, without the power
   The charms so near to touch.

Deceived.

HAST thou forgotten
  That hour of our parting,
When, thro' thy smiling,
  I saw thy tears starting,
And how in silence
  And rapture I trembled
To learn the dear secret
  No longer dissembled.

Friends were around us,
  So no vows were spoken,
No, none were uttered,
  But have none been broken ?
Or is the eye's language
  So false in expression
That from the lip only
  Can come true confession ?

Well, thou'st deceived me,
  I can forget it,
That I believed thee
  Shall I regret it ?
No ; for if ne'er in
  False hearts we confided,
Ne'er should we find where
  The true ones resided.

Only Children.

I KNEW thee in thy childhood,
   And dreamed but little then,
My playmate of the wildwood
   I ne'er should meet again.
'Twas well when with thee roaming
   In utter joy of heart,
I knew not times were coming
   When we should dwell apart.

Our loves were children's lovings,
   We seemed free of the earth,
I kissed thee in thy rovings,
   I kissed thee by thy hearth.
And none took heed to chide us,
   Ah me, it mattered not,
What cared they to divide us
   Who knew our future lot ?

To M—V.

THOSE happy hours on the Italian sea—
    Dost thou forget them ?
The nights you lingered there awake with me,
    Dost thou regret them ?
That when thy name I traced on the still deep.
    And as each letter
Vanished, I whispered " in my heart—I'll keep
    The record better."

Dost thou remember—and the windless day,
    Our barque lay sleeping,
When I looked up from reading that sweet lay
    Which set thee weeping—
Dost thou remember ?   Mayest thou not tell ?
    Yet, oh ! why ask thee,
Silence may sometimes be preserved *too* well,
    Thine eyes unmask thee.

Barbara Lyle.

I WONDER what's become
   Of pretty Barbara Lyle,
If any tears she's shed
   Since last I saw her smile.
I wonder if we'd loved
   If she would have been true ;
Or if a false heart lay
   Beneath those eyes of blue.

I wonder if the light
   From those blue eyes is gone,
Or if they're shining still,
   And whom they shine upon.
Perchance, a husband lays
   His head upon her breast,
Methinks a happy man
   On such sweet spot to rest !

'Tis strange on these old times
   We love so oft to gaze,
As if there were no joys
   In life's maturer days.
There sits my own beloved,
   My children round her smile ;
Why heed then what's become
   Of pretty Barbara Lyle ?

She's not for Me.

No, not for me—she's very fair, I own,
　　And fitting mate for those
Who woo a woman for her looks alone ;
　　And yet her looks disclose
More pride than beauty, a disdain of love,
The serpent smiles there, but without the dove.

What scorn and ridicule are in her speech !
　　Sad from the lips of youth—
Sad when they learn, still sadder when they teach
　　To love wit more than truth.
'Tis early time the cynic's part to play,
And shows both head and heart have gone astray.

And, in a maid, to womanhood scarce grown,
　　'Tis worse than premature ;
Who plucks a flower that's blighted ere 'tis blown
　　In hopes 'twill then grow pure ?
Not I for one, so, lady fair, we part,
I want not sneers and titters but—a heart !

Town and Country.

Give me no town—famed maiden,
　　Blazing at midnight ball,
With rings and jewels laden,
　　To hold my heart in thrall.
Rather, in rustic hamlet,
　　Tripping the fields along,
And with the murmuring streamlet
　　Mingling her own sweet song—
　　　　The maid I'd see
　　　　Who was for me.

Not she with curls e'er drooping
　　O'er each new novel's leaves,
Some idler o'er her stooping
　　To watch her bosom's heaves,
Is lady for my wooing :
　　Thinking but acting too,
Admiring less, than *doing*,
　　The beautiful and true,
　　　　The maid must be
　　　　Who is for me.

To M. G.

YEARS have gone by since last I strung
My harp for one so fair and young,
Nor sing I now as once I sung ;
    The days of stern reality
Have clouded o'er those visions bright
Which, in the dawn of manhood's light,
Gave to my thoughts, by day and night,
    A poet's ideality.

Yet tho' those visions fair have flown,
My harp has lost not all its tone,
It's minstrel is but wiser grown ;
    Not loving less the beautiful
But more enamoured of the true ;
Not watching less Heaven's skies of blue,
But walking this earth-pathway through
    With step more slow and dutiful.

With calmer eye I look around,
Pausing, at times, my harp to sound,
Wherever gentle hearts are found
    To listen ; but, ah, well-a-day !

The world's harsh voices are too strong
To suffer many mid the throng
To hear me, as I pass along,
    Pour out my simple melody.

But thou, sweet maiden, yet art free
From this heart-chilling apathy,
And willingly I wake for thee
    My harp : and though not movingly
As younger, warmer bards, I fling
My hands across each throbbing string,
It will not be in vain I sing,
    If thou but list approvingly.

Thou smilest—long may that fair brow
Keep bright and sorrowless as now ;
But all their trials have, and thou
    From thine hast no security ;
Truth to which none should wish thee blind,
Yet still, with tranquil heart and mind,
Thy duty in the present find,
    And leave to God futurity.

Quarrel of Friends.

THOSE bitter words *did* smite my heart,
　But thine by pain was not unriven,
For I was hasty; so let's part
　Alike forgiving and forgiven.
Nor let us struggle to forget
　This hour when next we come together,
But gladly think our friendship met,
　And bore, unharmed, such stormy weather.

The fairest garden, winds and showers
　Assail, yet leave it lovely still,
Doing the plants, whose leaves and flowers
　They scatter, no enduring ill.
So with our friendship, though it be
　By passing gusts awhile defruited,
But little harm is done the tree,
　Which stands too firm to be uprooted.

Life and Love.

To love and to be loved is not the whole
Of life's great purpose ; duty, self-control,
Demand diviner yearnings of the soul.

Two minds, two hearts, with one accordant thrill,
Make a fair picture—picture fairer still
Is one unbending, self-denying will.

Love is not virtue, prize it as we may,
But oft, when contradicted in its sway,
Drives virtue from, or stops it on, its way ;

Or, flowing smoothly, rounds us in a fence
Which makes us look on with indifference
All but its own small world of self and sense.

Life is our care ; let love come if it will,
Not held chief good, nor want of it chief ill ;
Accounted dear, but duty dearer still !

We Laugh at Love.

We laugh at love when youth is spent,
  Telling it, as a theme for jest,
When first *we* knew what passion meant,
  And how the secret thrilled our breast
When mid gay crowds, round us assembled,
Came she at whose dear voice we trembled,
And for the sake of whose sweet glance
Alone we cared to join the dance ;
Hoping, perchance, by no one heard,
To whisper some endearing word
That might, mid the surrounding stir,
Elicit haply one from her !
Yet, fearing what we dared avow,
  Might answer bring our hopes to shatter.
Well, such fears shade no more our brow,
And e'en may set us smiling now,
  But, ah ! 'twas then no laughing matter !

With wife and children round us, we
  Forget the days of our love-making,
And won't believe that hearts can be
  Brought by it to the verge of breaking.
We think such wounds will heal with time ;
That wedding early's half a crime,

Bringing more sorrow, toil, and care
Than love itself has strength to bear.
Chilling and false ! Come weal or woe,
Come state of fortune high or low,
Purely returned, and purely given,
Love still is man's best gift from Heaven.

Mine at Last.

MINE—mine at last ! Scarce hoped for hour
  Of sunshine on the abiding cloud
That seemed on my life's path to lour.
  What now are cares ? Oh, let them crowd
My heart, since there I hold *thee* fast,
My own—my own—mine—mine at last !

I cannot, in my new-found bliss,
  My many happy thoughts convey,
With the full sweetness of thy kiss
  Still on my lips, what could *they* say ?
Silently let me hold thee fast,
My own—my own—mine—mine at last !

The Soul's Soliloquy.

I.

SPIRIT, that to One alone
In thy inmost depths art known—
Pris'ner of the clayey cell,
In which thou, at birth, must dwell ;
Seed from heaven sent to grow
On this earthly soil below ;
Spite the weeds, with which 'tis rife,
Struggle through them into life !

II.

Sigh not that thine outward shape
Cannot doom of dust escape ;
Wear it so that men may view
Something brighter shining thro',
As a robe that fitly tells
Of the worth that 'neath it dwells,
Yet as destined at death's portal
To be changed for one immortal.

III.

Swift though Time's advance may be,
He no terrors has for thee ;
Centuries to thee of earth
Were but one continuous birth.

Age, that doth the body kill,
Thee with stronger life shall fill;
Called above or left below,
Still *thy* function is—to *grow*.

IV.

Grow—expanding every hour,
Into fuller, fairer, flower:
With the strength of love and duty,
Into wisdom, goodness, beauty;
Spreading nearer to the skies,
Till at length to heaven they rise;
Called to find a home above
In their God's eternal love.

The First Gold Rush at Melbourne.

"Declinat cursus, aurumque volubile tollit."

I.

How it moves us—how it proves us—
    This bewildering tale of gold!
How they glisten—how they listen—
    Eyes and ears when it is told!
How it sets us all a-raving,
How it sets us all a-craving,

Thinking of what might be got,
   If we were but on the spot !
Gone are many, some still linger,
   Waiting with unquiet heart,
And few feel not itching finger,
   As they see the rest depart,

II.

In the bush, and in the city,
" *Gold's* " the universal ditty,
Not alone the pauper—miser—
   Slaves of avarice or want,
But the wealthier and the wiser
   Seek for baptism at its font.
Men who'd think it a base libel,
   If 'twas hinted they were poor ;
Men who talk about their Bible,
   And plates hold at the church door—
Labour-hirer, working-man,
Clerk, mechanic, artisan,
Washed and unwashed—high and low,
Mingle in the current's flow
That doth to the " diggins " go.

III.

What is this strange scene we near,
New to eye and new to ear ?
See them delving there below,
Ev'ry dig a gamester's throw ;

What is this they pause to view—
Turning o'er and looking through?
Ha !—the glittering ore appears,
Gone are all their long-felt fears ;
Dig, my boys—behold, behold—
Dig away—for this *is* gold !

IV.

Look around on all the scene,
Much that's mournful doth it mean.
See how they eye one another,
Should thus brother look on brother ?
Yonder scowling visage mark,
Well it is not lone or dark,
For if murder could be done,
There, to do it, standeth one.

V.

Night is come, and here and there
Sleepers close their eyes in prayer ;
But 'neath more than one tarpaulin
There is drinking, gaming, brawling—
Ending oft in challenged fight
To be fought by Sabbath light,
If, perchance, the coming morn
Of a week-day should be born—
For e'en hatred can keep cold
Sooner than stop work for gold,
Digging for it, as if God
Had hid salvation 'neath the sod !

VI.

Gold ! supreme is thy dominion,
God of church upon whose creed
Every nation is agreed;
Where's another one on which
Holds mankind the same opinion—
'Tis expedient to be rich ?
Missionary in Christ's name,
Would but find reception tame,
By the side of him who came
Thy evangel to proclaim.
With a faith that never falters,
With a trust that heeds no shock
Millions kneel before thy altars,
Millions to thy temple flock.
Never yet was homage found
Unto King of earth or heaven
As to thee so freely given—
Thee the *monarch underground !*

Christmas in Australia.

I.

DECEMBER, yet not winter—but sunniest of skies,
A Christmas-day in summer! how strange to English
    eyes;
Strange—and a little sad too, for something seems away
That ought to be among us on this all-welcomed day.

II.

I miss the 'customed holly, o'er wall and window spread,
Its leaves so green and prickly, and its berries all so red,
The cheerful hearth at morning—more cheerful still at
    night,
When all sat round it chatting, nor wished for other light.

III.

Without too, as within, I miss signs of other times,
The singing of the carols, the ringing of the chimes;
The snow upon the grass-plot, the frost upon the trees,
One hardly feels 'tis Christmas without some signs like
    these.

IV.

And yet what doth it matter, when that blest time comes
    round,
What season is prevailing where Christian hearts are
    found?
Be summer or be winter, where falleth Christmas-day,
The Christmas of the *spirit* can be kept but *one* way.

V.

We may as in old England enjoy the festive cheer
That marks a merry Christmas—no lack of that is here,
Yet better were it absent from every Christian board,
Than sots or gluttons make us in honour of our Lord.

———◦◦———

Advance, Victoria !

I.

From crowded cities severed far
Where glitters bright the southern star
There lies a land of wide domains,
Of golden rocks, and grassy plains ;
Whose soil to till, and wealth unlock,
From distant climes, all peoples flock,
Whilst, canopied 'neath cloudless skies,
They help a mighty nation's rise.

II.

Victoria ! those domains are thine ;
As bright a sun may elsewhere shine,
And smile upon a fairer show
Of glories that with age must grow ;
But never yet was land more rife
With seeds that sprang to quicker life,
And never land of olden time
Gave promise of a richer prime.

III.

Advance, Victoria !—may'st thou be
As good and great as thou art free ;
Beware of the empoisoned fruit
That springs from Faction's deadly root,
No truth—howe'er distasteful—spurn,
But ear suspicious ever turn
To all who mouth high-sounding creeds,
But serve thee with no useful deeds.

IV.

Advance—with step more sure than swift,
Shun waste—shun also cramping thrift ;
Progressive, bold—but calm and just ;
Deceive no hopes—betray no trust,
Despite each current's hostile force,
Like river strong—hold on thy course,
Seeking thy goal with forward tide
That naught can stop, or turn aside.

THE END.

London : SMITH, ELDER AND Co., 15½, Old Bailey, E.C.

www.ingramcontent.com/pod-product-compliance
Lightning Source LLC
Chambersburg PA
CBHW031106020726
47495CB00007B/2074